She lifted her hand to knock again, but the door was yanked open, startling her enough that she actually fell back a step.

Annoyed with herself, she stiffened her shoulders as she looked up into the face of the man who stood there.

Six feet tall. A lean one-seventy. Dark hair. Dark brow, dark beard. Her brain automatically categorized the details that she'd only so far seen on a Department of Motor Vehicles record.

When she got to the eyes, though?

She felt her brain short-circuit.

Not blue.

Not green.

Aqua.

Entirely heart-stopping, even though they were glaring at her.

"I can't believe I finally found you," she blurted.

His lips thinned. "It's my only one." He shoved a hardcover book into her hands. "Now get off my property." Before she could blink, he slammed the door shut. Right in her face.

She was actually too stunned to react.

At first.

RETURN TO THE DOUBLE C:
Under the big blue Wyoming sky,
this family discovers true love

Dear Reader,

Ali Templeton has always felt a little inferior to her siblings. They all excelled in school. She was average. They are professionals. She's a cop. But what she's never doubted was that her parents loved them all equally. Without question. So she knows her occasional sense of inferiority is just something inside her—something *she* needs to overcome. Grant Cooper, on the other hand, has not spent his entire life within a loving, supportive family. Outwardly, he excelled in a lot of areas—including the military. What he doesn't know inwardly, however, is how to overcome *his* sense of unworthiness. For him, it's easier to believe he's meant to be alone.

Fortunately, his world and Ali's collide and from that moment on, their lives change. She recognizes the man he is inside so well that eventually, her love helps Grant recognize it, too. And he realizes that *not* being alone is the most worthwhile risk of all.

Happy reading!

Allison

Show Me a Hero

Allison Leigh

HARLEQUIN® SPECIAL EDITION

Recycling programs
for this product may
not exist in your area.

ISBN-13: 978-1-335-46592-4

Show Me a Hero

HARLEQUIN®
www.Harlequin.com

Printed in U.S.A.

Though her name is frequently on bestseller lists, **Allison Leigh**'s high point as a writer is hearing from readers that they laughed, cried or lost sleep while reading her books. She credits her family with great patience for the time she's parked at her computer, and for blessing her with the kind of love she wants her readers to share with the characters living in the pages of her books. Contact her at allisonleigh.com.

For my family.

Chapter One

The house was nineteen-point-six miles outside of town.

"Incredible," Ali Templeton muttered under her breath when she pulled up in front of the dated-looking two-story building that sat on a small knoll in what seemed like the middle of nowhere.

Only nineteen-point-six miles.

She exhaled and pushed open the door of her cruiser, sticking one sturdy boot out onto the frozen red earth. She was on personal time and probably shouldn't be using the vehicle assigned to her by the department. It would be one more reason for her sergeant to give her grief, but her own little pickup truck was in the shop, and would be remaining there until she could scrabble together the money to pay for the new transmission it needed.

She zipped up her jacket against the whistling wind

as she studied the house in front of her. Sgt. Gowler had been annoyed with her ever since she stopped dating his son, so she was used to it by now. What was one more reprimand?

Discovering that Grant Cooper was living just nineteen-point-six miles outside of her very own hometown was either the height of irony, or the proof that she wasn't much of a cop, just like Sgt. Gowler seemed to think.

Not that she was here for professional reasons.

Not exactly.

Her bangs blew into her face, obscuring her view, and she shoved her sunglasses up onto the top of her head to keep her hair out of her eyes. She should never have impetuously cut the bangs. It was taking forever for them to grow long enough to stay contained in the bun she had to wear because Gowler was a stickler for regulations.

She'd been out to this abandoned ranch once before. Just over a year ago. Then, it had been at the behest of a single mom at her wit's end over the wild crowd her fifteen-year-old son had fallen in with. Alongside one of the county's deputy sheriffs, she'd rounded up Trevor and the rest of the kids, boarded up the broken windows that had allowed them access to the vacant house and hauled the kids back home to their parents.

There were still no animals in the fields. But now the sheets of plywood were gone. All the windows were intact. And though there was no sign of any vehicles, there was a thin stream of smoke coming from the chimney that she hoped meant the man she sought was actually inside.

When she went up the weathered porch steps, they creaked ominously, as if they hadn't borne the weight of a human being in about half a century. Jabbing her gloved finger against the doorbell didn't elicit any response, so she tugged off the glove, balled her fingers into a fist and pounded loudly on the door. A shelf of snow slid off the roof, landing with a plop next to her feet.

She wasn't going to take it as a bad sign. The snow could just have easily landed on her head.

She swiped the pile sideways with her boot until it fell off the side of the small porch, and knocked again, a little more gently this time. Even if he didn't answer the door, she wasn't going to give up.

Not now that she'd finally found him.

She glanced at her watch. She couldn't afford to be too long before she reported in, or Gowler really would have a legitimate reason to be all over her case. But she'd just discovered where Grant Cooper was and she wasn't taking any chances. She knocked on the door again, then glanced over her shoulder, scanning the landscape around the house. It looked even more desolate than it had when she'd rousted the weed-smoking teenagers.

But then again, it was the middle of January. In the middle of Wyoming.

"Come on." She lifted her hand to knock again, but the door was yanked open from the inside, startling her enough that she fell back a step.

Annoyed with herself, she stiffened her shoulders and looked up into the face of the man who stood there.

Six feet tall. A lean 170. Dark-haired. Dark-browed, dark-bearded. Her brain automatically categorized the details that she'd only seen in a photo in his DMV record.

When she got to the eyes, though?

She felt her brain short-circuit.

Not blue.

Not green.

Aqua.

Entirely heart-stopping, even though they *were* glaring at her.

"I can't believe I finally found you," she blurted.

His lips thinned. "It's my only one." He shoved something into her hands. "Now get off my property." Before she could blink, he slammed the door shut. Right in her face.

She was too stunned to react.

At first.

But annoyance quickly hit and she pounded on the door again, using the spine of the hardback book he'd pushed into her hand. It served one good purpose at least—it made an effective door-knocker.

It didn't matter to her if he turned out to be as strange as a three-dollar bill. She wasn't going to just turn around and leave because he hadn't greeted her with a big smile and howdy-do.

So she banged with the book and pulled out her badge with her other hand. "Mr. Cooper, open the door," she said loudly. "I'm not going away until we've had a chance to speak." She banged again. "Open up!"

The door was yanked open again. "If Chelsea sent you—"

Ali did the shoving this time and pushed her badge right in front of his face. "I'm Officer Templeton with the Braden Police Department, here on official business." She was definitely stretching the truth about that, but oh, well. "I don't know who Chelsea is, nor do I care, unless she has information about the whereabouts of Daisy Miranda."

Only because she was watching him closely did she catch the glint of surprise in his otherwise glowering expression.

"Are you Grant Cooper?"

He still looked like he wasn't going to answer and she wiggled her badge a little, even as she tried to make herself as physically imposing as five foot two could ever be.

"Yes," he admitted through his teeth.

"Then Daisy is your sister." The woman might be a rolling stone, never staying in one place for more than three or four months at a time, but she seemed to have tried to always maintain some sort of contact with her brother.

Which was the only reason Ali had found him right here at all. She'd literally followed a postcard to the man.

Nineteen-point-six miles. He'd been practically under her nose all this time.

His expression darkened even more. "My sister's name is *Karen Cooper*. Not Daisy Miranda."

But he'd recognized the name. Ali had seen it in his eyes. She wished they had a photo of Daisy. But she didn't. Just a general description provided by the people who'd known her during her brief stay in Braden. "Medium height. Slender. Red hair, green eyes? Maybe she married?"

His expression revealed his disbelief. "No way."

"Does she often use an alias? Are there other names she goes by?"

His lips were pressed together.

She let out a little breath of frustration. "If you think your silence will make me give up, you're wrong, Mr.

Cooper. Regardless of what she's calling herself these days, I'm looking for her. And I intend to find her."

"You and about a dozen others. If you're here because my sister owes somebody money, you're out of luck. You won't get it from me."

"This isn't about money."

"I don't care what it's about." He tried closing the door again, only to glare at her even harder when he couldn't because she'd quickly planted her heavy boot in the doorway.

"So you don't care about her abandoned baby?" Ordinarily, she would have cringed a little at her own bluntness, but these weren't ordinary circumstances.

This time she didn't have to look closely to see the shock that crossed his handsome face. He closed his aqua eyes for a second. Then he frowned and moved away from the doorway. But he didn't try shutting the door.

It was invitation enough for her and she stepped inside.

The interior of the house was only slightly less derelict than it had been when she'd confronted the teenagers. Then, the kids had been sprawled around on sleeping bags and tattered beach chairs. Now, only one piece of furniture remained in the main room—a couch that was presumably new, considering the thick plastic wrapped around it. It was pushed to one side of the square room and sat beneath a foggy-glassed wall mirror. A couple of packing boxes were stacked next to it, along with what appeared to be new, unfinished kitchen cabinets. On the other side of the room were gallon cans of paint along with paint rollers stacked atop a tarp. Clearly he was preparing to paint over the graffiti-covered walls.

The problems she and her sister were having with the Victorian they'd been restoring were owed strictly to the age and decline of the house. He had to deal with an old house *plus* neglect and outright vandalism.

He disappeared through a door near the paint cans and she followed, setting the thick book on top of one of the boxes as she passed the stack.

He was standing in the middle of the kitchen, seeming to stare at nothing at all.

He made no sign that he even recognized her presence. Chewing the inside of her cheek, she stepped around him to reach the sink against the cabinetless wall. When she'd been here before, the kitchen had had vile yellow cabinets and she wondered if he'd pulled them out in preparation for the new ones, or if it had been vandals.

The white enamel sink was still chipped, but it was no longer filled with cigarette ashes and discarded beer cans. In fact, it looked scrupulously clean. There was a dish drainer sitting on the bottom of the sink and she pulled one of the glasses from it. It was still damp from being recently washed, and she filled it with water.

He hadn't moved a muscle.

"Mr. Cooper, why don't you sit down?" She gestured to the round table wedged in the space between an avocado-green refrigerator and a tin-doored pantry cupboard.

He still didn't move.

His chambray shirtsleeves were rolled up his sinewy forearms and she cautiously touched his elbow through the cloth.

He jerked as if she'd prodded him with an electric rod and glared down at her.

She pushed the water glass toward him until he had

no choice but to take it. "Maybe this will help," she said calmly despite the distraction of his intensely colored eyes. "Would you mind if I sat?"

His eyebrows lowered as she pulled out one of the padded metal chairs without waiting for his answer. She sat on the edge of the yellow vinyl cushion, hoping he would follow suit.

She needed his cooperation. It would be easier to get that if she could get beyond his annoyance and his shock. In her experience, sitting together at someone's kitchen table was a step in the right direction.

After a brief hesitation, he pulled out a second chair. The metal legs scraped against the black-and-white checkered linoleum floor. He sat, and finally drank down half the water.

Then he set the glass in the middle of the table and sighed. He rested his forearms on the Formica and pressed his fingers together until the tips turned white around his short, neatly clipped fingernails. "I didn't know she'd had a baby," he said after a moment. His voice was low. Gruff. "Or that she was in Braden. We—" He broke off and cleared his throat, curling his fingers into fists. "We haven't spoken in a while."

Ali very nearly reached out to cover his hands with her own. Instead, she clasped them together in her lap just to be sure she kept them under control. She wanted to ask what his and his sister's connection was to Braden that they'd both ended up here during entirely different time frames. Braden was simply too small for it to be coincidental. But she held back that particular question for now. "How long is a while?"

His jaw shifted. "A while." He focused those unsettling eyes on her face. "How do you know this baby you're talking about is Karen's?"

She couldn't fudge the facts about that. "I don't know for certain that she is," she admitted. "Only that a child has been abandoned, and the evidence seems to point to her being Karen's."

"What evidence?"

An old-fashioned electric clock hung on the wall opposite them, above the stove. It was shaped like a black cat, with a long tail that swung right and left in time with the ticking hands of the clock face on the cat's belly. "There was an unsigned note left along with the infant. We believe your sister wrote it. Her wording was distinct."

His eyebrows rose slightly.

"'Jaxie, please take care of Layla for me.'" Ali recited the brief missive from memory.

Grant sat back in his chair. His expression turned annoyed again. "How does that tell you anything? Except the kid's name is Layla. You don't even know for sure that the author of the note is Layla's mother. You're just assuming."

"In the absence of any other information, it's the only assumption we have to make. Maybe Daisy isn't—"

"Karen."

"*Karen.* Maybe she isn't the baby's mother, but she clearly had some involvement with the child or she wouldn't have written the note."

"*If* she wrote the note. Do you even have proof of that? And who the hell is Jaxie?"

She glanced at the clock again. Gowler would take lateness even worse than he would her personal use of a department vehicle. God only knew what he would assign her to next. Janitorial, maybe. It was about the one thing he hadn't done. Yet. "Maybe I should start at the beginning."

He gave her a long look that seemed to say "you think?" "Maybe you should."

She suddenly felt too warm and unzipped her jacket. "An infant was left on the doorstep of a home owned by two brothers in Braden last month. The only identifying item left with the baby was the note. Unsigned, as I said. On common, white paper. No clear fingerprints. But the reference to Jaxie presumably meant Jaxon Swift, who is one of the occupants of the home. Mr. Swift owns a business in Braden and he had an employee for a short while named—" she inclined her head slightly "—Daisy Miranda, who was the only one who ever used that nickname for him. But she left Mr. Swift's employment more than a year ago and he hasn't heard from her since."

"So? The kid is his. Why else leave her for him? What's the problem?" His eyes looked cynical. "*Jaxie* doesn't want to take responsibility?"

"That was our assumption, too, at first. That he was the father, I mean. But DNA tests have already disproved his paternity. He's not Layla's father. The business Mr. Swift owns is a bar. Magic Jax. Karen was a cocktail waitress. Their uniforms are, um—"

"Skimpy?"

She hesitated. She'd been known to work as a cocktail waitress at Magic Jax a time or two for extra money. She was taking a few shifts right now to help get her car out of auto-shop jail. "Let's just say the outfits are closely fitted. Given the timing, it's unlikely that your sister was even pregnant when she quit working there. There are no records locally about Layla's birth, but we estimate she's now about three months old."

"So where is the baby?"

Ali kept herself from shifting. "The judge in charge

of her case has placed her temporarily with a local family while we investigate."

His lips twisted. "He's put her in foster care, you mean."

The term was accurate, but implied a formality and distance that wasn't the case at all, since it was Ali's own sister Maddie and her new husband, Lincoln Swift, who were providing the care. "Yes. A very good foster family. Can you give me any information about Karen's friends? If she was involved with a particular man?"

"No. I didn't even know she'd been here in Wyoming."

Ali waited a moment for him to explain further, but he didn't. And even though she tried to give him her best demanding stare, his gaze didn't shy away.

She was afraid that she was the one who came away feeling unsteady. She wasn't used to feeling unnerved by a man. Even an unreasonably handsome one.

Determined to get back on track, she reached into the inner pocket of her jacket and pulled out one of her business cards. They were generic cards for the police department, but she kept a small supply on which she'd added her badge number, email and phone number. "If there's anything that comes to you, anything at all, please consider calling me."

He didn't take the card. "So you can arrest her for abandoning her child?"

She thought about the sweet baby that she herself had rocked and played with and fallen for just like everyone else who'd come into Layla's orbit. It didn't really matter what had drawn this man and his nomadic sister to the same place at entirely different times.

What mattered was Layla.

She placed the card on the center of the table as she

stood. "So I can find a child's mother," she amended quietly.

He didn't respond. Didn't reach for the card.

She squelched a sigh. "Thank you for your time, Mr. Cooper." She turned to leave the kitchen.

"I haven't talked to Karen in nearly three years," he said abruptly.

She stopped and looked at him. She couldn't imagine not speaking with any one of her siblings for three days, much less three years. "That's a long time."

"You don't know Karen." He stood from the table and escorted her from the barren kitchen back through the nonlivable living room. "She's flighty. Irresponsible. Manipulative. But she wouldn't have done this." He opened the front door and a rush of bitterly cold wind swept inside. "She wouldn't have dumped off her baby."

"Not even if she was desperate?"

His lips tightened. "If she was that desperate, she would have let me know."

"Well…" Ali zipped up her jacket. Fortunately, her departmental SUV had good heating. She stuck out her hand, hoping to show him that she wasn't his adversary. "If you think of anything at all that might help us find her, please consider calling me."

He looked vaguely resigned. He briefly clasped her hand, then shoved his fingers in the front pockets of his jeans. "I won't think of anything."

She fought the urge to tuck away her own hand, because her palm was most definitely singing. "But if you do—"

"But if I do, I'll contact you."

It was the best she could do at the moment. Bringing up the subject of testing *his* DNA to help identify whether or not Karen, aka Daisy Miranda, was actually Layla's mother wouldn't get her anywhere. Not just yet. She didn't have to possess the kind of brilliant mind that had been bestowed on her siblings to recognize that particular fact. "Thank you." She barely took two steps out the front door when it closed solidly behind her.

She didn't look back, but let out a long, silent exhale that clouded visibly around her head as she went down the steps and headed to the SUV. At least she'd learned Daisy's real name.

Daisy Miranda might have seemed to have disappeared off the face of the earth.

But maybe Karen Cooper hadn't.

She pulled open the truck door and climbed inside, quickly turning on the ignition and the heat.

Only when she drove away did she finally rub her palm against the side of her pants until the tingling went away.

Grant Cooper watched the SUV until it was out of sight.

Then he turned on his heel and strode through the disaster zone that was the living room, heading back to the kitchen.

The sight of the book sitting on top of his packing crates stopped him.

He picked up the thick novel. Stared for a moment at the slick black cover featuring an embossed outline of a soldier. The author's name, T. C. Grant, was spelled out in gold and was as prominent as the title—*CCT Final Rules*.

He turned and threw the book—hard—across the room.

It bounced against the plaster wall, knocked a can of white paint onto its side and fell with a thud to the floor.

He still felt like punching something.

If not for Karen, he never would have written the damn book he'd just thrown. But what was a little signature forgery, which had locked him into writing a fourth *CCT Rules* book, compared to abandoning her own child?

He raked his fingers through his hair.

"She wouldn't do that," he muttered.

But his eyes caught in the old mirror hanging on the wall. And there was uncertainty in his reflection.

Karen would have *had* to have been desperate to do it. If he hadn't barred her from his life three years ago, she'd have come to him.

Just like she'd always come to him, expecting him to clean up the latest mess that she'd landed herself in.

Until that last, unforgiveable act, when she'd signed his name on the publishing contract he'd decided against accepting, he'd always been there for her.

She'd been crashing on his couch at the time, pitching the advantages of the contract as heavily as his publisher had been. It was his fault for leaving the unsigned contract right out on his desk where she'd had easy access to it. His fault for not even realizing the contract had disappeared, until he'd received it back, fully executed and with a handwritten note of "glad to see you came to your senses" attached. That's what he got for having an ex-wife for his publisher. He'd known immediately what Karen had done, then. Signed his name on the dotted line. Same as she'd used to sign their parents' names on school report cards.

It was easier to write the book than admit what she'd done. Courtesy of his ex-wife, Karen had walked away with a shopping spree for her part in "convincing" him to take the deal he'd admittedly been waffling over.

She'd never known that writing the book had taken everything he had left out of him. Because he'd drawn the line with her by then. No more cleaning up. No more paying off. He didn't want to hear from her. Didn't want her phone calls. Her text messages. Her emails. Not even the postcards she always mailed from the places she ended up on her never-ending quest to find her "perfect" life.

Didn't matter how many times Grant told her there was no such thing. His troubled sister was always on the hunt for it.

She'd even come to Wyoming, where she didn't have any connections at all except for the one that he had.

And now there was a baby. Supposedly hers.

He looked in the mirror.

It wasn't his reflection he saw, though. It was his sister's face when he'd told her to stay out of his life for good.

He looked away from the mirror. Sighed deeply.

"Hell, Karen. What have you done?"

Chapter Two

Grant didn't recognize her at first.

Which wasn't all that surprising, he supposed.

Instead of the shapeless navy blue police uniform covering her from neck to ankles, she wore a short red dress edged in black, which crossed tightly over her breasts to tie in a bow at her hip, and high-heeled black shoes. Her shapely legs peeked out below the snug hem that reached only a few inches past her butt.

He studied Officer Templeton over the rim of his beer as she made her way between tables, taking orders and picking up empties on her way toward the bar, where he was sitting in front of the taps. She didn't even glance his way when she got to the end of the bar, delivered her orders to the bartender and picked up a fresh set of drinks.

"Thanks, Marty," she said as she headed back out to the tables with her heavy tray balanced on one hand.

Grant's gaze followed the sway of her hips longer than was probably polite before he managed to pull it away.

The bartender was back at the taps, filling more beer mugs. He smiled wryly as he caught Grant's eyes. "Don't waste your time on that one," he advised. "The trips are hard to catch."

"Trips?"

"There are two more, look just like her. Identical triplets. Except one of them got married a couple weeks ago."

"I guess at least she got caught."

Marty grinned. "Yeah, by the richest guy in town. Lincoln Swift. His brother, Jax, owns this place."

Grant's interest was piqued a little more. Officer Templeton hadn't provided that particular piece of information. That her brother-in-law's *brother* owned the bar where Karen had worked. Or that she herself worked there, too. Because the police department didn't pay enough, or because of some other secret she harbored?

He glanced over his shoulder again. It was easy to follow Officer Templeton's progress around the dimly lit room. For one, the dress was like a bright red beacon. Then there was her hair. She didn't have it twisted back in a god-awful tight bun tonight; instead, it reached beyond her shoulders, a streaky mass of brown and blond waves that bounced as she walked.

Seymour would have taken one look at Officer Templeton and said she was sex on a stick.

If Seymour wasn't six feet under.

Grant looked back into his beer. He didn't want to think about Seymour Reid any more than he wanted to speculate about his sister and her baby. But Seymour had been on his mind ever since he'd gotten the invitation in the mail that afternoon.

It was for a ceremony a month from now, when Claudia, Seymour's widow, would accept the Distinguished Service Cross for her deceased husband. She'd included a handwritten note for Grant, imploring him to attend. Grant had been Seymour's best friend. He was godfather to their two children. Wouldn't he please, *please* come to North Carolina, where the ceremony was being held?

He dug his fingertips into his pounding temples. Unlike Grant, who'd been a combat controller with the US Air Force, Seymour had been army all the way. A Green Beret. He'd been a few years older than Grant, a hothead with the need to be a hero running in his veins. Grant had been attached to Sey's unit for more than half the time he'd served. When he'd gotten out of the air force nearly six years ago because he'd thought it would save his marriage, Seymour had warned him it wouldn't. At the time, Grant had warned Seymour that *his* marriage wouldn't survive *him* staying in.

But it turned out Seymour had been right.

As usual.

Grant and Chelsea had been divorced within a year.

At Seymour's funeral last year, Claudia's wedding ring had been firmly in place on her finger.

"Getcha another, bud?"

He realized Marty had spoken and looked at his now-empty mug. He hadn't even realized he'd finished the beer.

Which was a pretty good reason not to have another. "No thanks." He tossed enough cash on the bar to cover the drink and a tip, then pushed out of his seat and grabbed his coat from the empty bar stool next to him.

From the corner of his eye, he saw Officer Templeton bending over slightly as she cleared a table. How anyone as short as her could have legs that went on forever was beyond him. His ex-wife was nearly as tall as he was and her legs hadn't seemed that long.

He was almost to the door when the pretty police officer straightened and her gaze collided with his.

She looked surprised for about half a second, then dumped her round tray into the hands of one of her customers and started toward him, not stopping until she was two feet away. She propped her hands on her slender hips and gave him a steady look. "There are at least ten bars in this town. Yet you pick Magic Jax."

"So?"

She shrugged. "Don't expect me to believe it's coincidental. You wanted to see the place where Daisy worked."

"Karen. And interesting that you didn't mention you work here, too."

"It's temporary." Her dark eyes continued to boldly meet his. "Are you going to ask when you can meet your niece?"

He grimaced. "You don't know that she's my niece. You only think she is."

"Little lady, are we gonna get our cocktails anytime soon, or—"

She looked at the old guy wearing a ten-gallon hat who'd just interrupted them. "Squire Clay, I've warned you before. If you call me 'little lady' again, I'm not gonna let you off for speeding the next time I stop you."

The auburn-haired woman with Ten Gallon hid a snicker.

"You want your drinks right this second, go on over and get 'em from Marty," she told him.

Ten Gallon looked a little abashed. "Sorry, Ali," he muttered.

Seeming satisfied, Officer Templeton looked back at Grant. "It's a pretty good hunch," she continued as if there'd been no interruption at all. "If you're willing to provide a DNA sample, we could know for sure."

His DNA wouldn't prove squat, though he had no intention of telling her that. Particularly now that they'd become the focus of everyone inside the bar. The town had a whopping population of 5,000. Maybe. It was small, but that didn't mean there wasn't a chance he'd be recognized. And the last thing he wanted was a rabid *CCT Rules* fan showing up on his doorstep.

He'd had too much of that already. It was one of the reasons he'd taken refuge at the ranch that his biological grandparents had once owned. He'd picked it up for a song when it was auctioned off years ago, but he hadn't seriously entertained doing much of anything with it— especially living there himself.

At the time, he'd just taken perverse pleasure in being able to buy up the place where he'd never been welcomed while they'd been alive.

Now, it was in such bad disrepair that to stay there even temporarily, he'd been forced to make it habitable.

He wondered if Karen had stayed there, unbeknownst to him. If she was responsible for any of the graffiti or the holes in the walls.

He pushed away the thought and focused on the officer. "Ali. What's it short for?"

She hesitated, obviously caught off guard. "Alicia, but nobody ever calls me that." He'd been edging closer to the door, but she'd edged right along with him. "So, about that—"

Her first name hadn't been on the business card she'd left for him. "Ali fits you better than Alicia."

She gave him a look from beneath her just-from-bed sexy bangs. "Stop changing the subject, Mr. Cooper."

"Start talking about something else, then. Better yet—" he gestured toward the bar and Marty "—start doing the job for *Jaxie* that you conveniently didn't mention before."

"I told you. It's temporary."

"I don't care if it is or isn't. But it makes me wonder what other details you've left out."

She looked annoyed. "Mr. Cooper—"

"G'night, Officer Ali." He pushed open the door and headed out into the night.

Ali stifled a curse as she watched Grant Cooper flip up the collar of his coat before he strode across the street.

Then the door to Magic Jax swung closed, cutting off the sight of him as well as the flow of cold air.

That didn't stop her from feeling shivery, though.

"Ali, all your orders are backing up."

She smiled at the other cocktail waitress working that night. It wasn't Charlene's fault that Ali was more interested in chasing after Grant Cooper for information about his sister than she was delivering drinks. "Sorry about that, Charlene." She couldn't push Grant out of her mind, but she could at least do what she was being paid to do. She hurried over to the bar and began loading up a tray. "Marty, you work most nights, right?"

The bartender didn't stop polishing glasses with his towel. "Most."

"Has he been in here before? Grant Cooper?"

"That's the guy you were just talking to?" Marty shrugged. "He's been in a couple times."

"Recently?"

"Yeah, I guess. The last few weeks, anyway."

"He ask any questions?"

Marty smiled wryly. "Yeah, what've we got on tap."

"About something *other* than beer?"

He shook his head. "Nope. Why? What's the story?"

"No story. I was just curious."

"You're never *just* curious, little... Ali," Squire interjected, stopping next to the bar and handing her a twenty. Not too long ago, she'd learned that the prosperous rancher from Weaver was sort of her relative. "Gloria and I are headin' out now."

Ali held up the twenty-dollar bill between two fingers. "What's this?"

"Bribery. For next time you pull me over for speeding."

"I've got a better idea, Squire." She plucked the hat off his gray head and tucked the twenty into the hatband. "Just stop speeding."

He guffawed and clapped her on the back with one of his big, rough hands. "You're a good girl, Ali, even if you got that uppity shrew for a granny. Ya oughta be finding a husband like that sis of yours has now."

She shook her head. "Nobody left who's worth marrying, Squire, since you've been hitched to Gloria all these years."

Standing near the doorway, Gloria sniffed loudly. "You're welcome to the old coot, Ali," she called. "You just say the word."

"Eh, she needs a young buck like that fella she was just talkin' to." Squire winked at her as he headed toward his wife and the exit. "Someone who can keep up with her."

Ali chuckled as was expected of her, and picked up the heavy tray.

But the truth was, she was thirty years old. She'd been dating since she was sixteen, and in all that time, she'd never met a man she'd been inclined to marry. And even though there'd been all sorts of inclinations circling inside her since she'd met Grant Cooper, none of them were in the "proper" realm of marriage.

As for her thoughts of Grant inhabiting an improper realm? Now that was a whole different kettle of fish.

But it was a lot more important to get Grant Cooper on board when it came to finding his sister than it was to think about properly improper-ing him.

She finished delivering the drinks and returned to load up her tray again.

"You going to work again tomorrow night?" Marty had pulled out the schedule and set it next to the drink station.

She sighed. The thought of spending another five hours wearing high heels held no appeal whatsoever, particularly after spending eight hours on her feet doing traffic duty, which was Gowler's latest punishment for her. But she still needed to get her truck out of the shop. "Yeah. And probably the night after that, if I can."

Marty scribbled on the schedule with his pencil. "You got it, little lady."

She made a face and tossed a lemon curl at him. "Very funny."

"I thought so." He grinned. "So what *is* behind your curiosity with that guy, Grant? Been a while since you dumped Keith Gowler. You finally looking for some fresh flesh?"

"Don't be gross, Marty." She preferred not to think that she'd *dumped* Keith since they'd only dated a few weeks, but it was true she'd been the one to put the brakes on dating him. "Grant might be a link to Layla."

Looking surprised, Marty stopped what he was doing. Most everyone in town, and particularly those who worked at the bar, knew a baby had been abandoned on the Swift brothers' doorstep last month. "He's the baby's father?"

"Uncle. He's Daisy Miranda's brother."

He propped his elbows on the bar. "No kidding. First time he came in, he told me he was staying at the old Carmody place outside of town."

"I know that *now*, so don't rub it in, okay?" Ali had been to New Mexico, Colorado, Idaho and California—all on her own time and Linc's pennies—following the circuitous trail that Daisy Miranda had left in her wake after quitting her job at Magic Jax. What Ali had learned along the way was that there had been only two consistent things about Daisy. One—her inconsistency. And two—her habit of sending postcards to a man named Grant Cooper that were routinely marked "return to sender." But one of those postcards had gone against that trend. It had been returned to the post office right here in Braden with a label on it containing a forwarding address for a desolate ranch located nineteen-point-six miles outside of town.

"Did you ever meet the Carmodys?" Marty pulled a tray of clean glasses from the dishwasher and started emptying it. "Roger and Helen?"

Ali shook her head. "I don't recall, but I suppose our paths would have probably crossed somewhere along the way. Can't really live in Braden all your life and not have run into everyone else." She nabbed one of the glasses, filled it with water and gulped it down. She hadn't had time to eat between her shift at the police department and when she'd gone on duty at Magic Jax, and her stomach was growling in the worst way. "I assume you did." Since he knew their names and all.

"They went to the same church as my grandma. Helen died way before he did." He made a face. "I think they were as uptight as my grandma, too."

"Well, I don't know anything about that. But I do know the bank took back Roger Carmody's property about ten years ago and he was forced to move away. I did not know, until just this week, however, that it had been bought at auction by none other than Grant Cooper, who turns out to be the brother of Daisy Miranda. He never lived there, though. Until now. He's got his work cut out for him. Leaving it vacant all those years was just an invitation for vandals." She set her glass in the rack of dirty dishes. "He's here and claiming he doesn't know anything about his sister's whereabouts or her baby."

"You don't believe him?"

Did she? Ali picked up her loaded tray again. "I think it's a lot of coincidences."

"In other words, you don't believe him."

There was something about Grant Cooper that made her instinctively want to believe him.

Or maybe it was just those darned aqua eyes.

"It's too soon to tell, Marty. It's just too soon to tell."

Eighteen hours later, Ali was working her way along Central Avenue, trying to pretend her feet hadn't turned into blocks of ice despite her boots as she monitored the frost-rimmed parking meters lining the four blocks of the downtown area. Since it had been snowing steadily since that morning, she didn't feel particularly inclined to punish the folks who didn't want to keep running out

to feed coins into the meters every ninety minutes. But
she also knew if she didn't write at least a few parking
tickets, Gowler would accuse her of being soft. And
being "soft" wasn't going to earn her an opportunity
to move up the ranks—assuming he ever forgave her
for dumping his son.

So she kept tramping up and down the snowy street
looking for the worst of the offenders. She pulled out
her pad and halfheartedly wrote out a couple citations,
tucking them beneath windshield wipers before shoving her cold hands back into her gloves.

When she reached the edge of the business district,
she crossed the quiet street and started making her way
back down the other side. For every two meters with
time on the clock, there were two more that had expired.
She tucked her nose farther into the knit scarf wound
around her neck and kept walking.

"Templeton!"

She stiffened at the sound of her name and looked
toward the source. Sgt. Gowler was standing on the
sidewalk in front of the library. She stomped her feet
in place on the sidewalk. "Yes, sir?"

"Know for a fact that meter you just passed is expired."

"By only a few minutes."

"Expired is expired."

She swallowed her retort and pulled her citation book
out of her pocket again. "Yes, sir."

It was obvious that he intended to stand there and wait
to make sure she did her duty. She turned back to the last
vehicle and peeled off her thick glove again so she could
write out the parking ticket. "Parking shmarking," she
muttered under her breath.

If she had more than a few bucks in change to spare,

she'd have carried it around in her pockets just to feed the dang meters herself. She tore the ticket off her pad and brushed the mound of snow off the windshield, then lifted the wiper enough to stick the ticket underneath it.

From the corner of her eye, she saw her boss go back inside the library.

Grumbling under her breath, she moved to the next expired meter next to a badly rusted truck. Her fingers were numb as she quickly marked the form and wrote in the license plate number. She yanked off the form and hurriedly shoved it under the wiper blade.

"You've gotta be kidding me."

She jerked up her head, looking toward the library again. But instead of Sgt. Gowler, this time it was Grant Cooper who'd come out onto the sidewalk.

He wore a dark jacket, unzipped, as if he was impervious to the weather that was currently making her long for life in the tropics. He had no scarf. Wore no gloves. Within seconds, his dark hair was dusted with snow. "I had ninety minutes on that thing," he said, pointing a long finger at the meter. "I haven't been in the library that long."

"The meters don't lie." She blew on her fingers, warming them a little before stuffing them back inside her glove. She wanted to tell him that if it was up to her, the meters wouldn't even exist on that street. They hadn't been updated in the past generation and the town had an old repair guy on standby just to keep them in operation. But she also didn't want her sergeant coming out again and seeing her flagrantly disregarding his instructions, either.

"Looks like you had a productive visit." She gestured at the stack of books he was carrying. The book he'd pushed into her hands when she'd shown up at his door wasn't far from her mind, though she'd paid no attention whatsoever to it at the time. "You must be a big reader."

He showed her one cover. "*Plumbing for Dummies*. Not exactly pleasure reading."

"Ah." She couldn't help a surprised laugh, as she shifted from one frozen stump to the other. "I actually need a copy of that one myself. My sisters and I own an old Victorian that we're restoring."

"Because you don't have enough to do, slinging drinks and doling out parking tickets?" He moved past her and tugged the ticket free. "How much is this gonna cost me?"

She started to point at the street sign nearby that warned of the fine for parking violations, only to realize that the surface of it was obscured by icy snow. "Fifty bucks. If you don't pay it by the date indicated on the ticket, the fine doubles. And it gets worse from there." Considering the state of his ranch house and the state of the vehicle, she hoped he got the message. Even if it was outrageously high, paying the parking fine on time was the simplest way to avoid owing even more money.

"Nice payback, Officer." The truck door screeched when he yanked it open and he tossed the ticket and his stack of books inside on the bench seat that was covered with a worn woven blanket. Maybe to keep his admittedly fine tushy warm or, if he was like Ali with her truck, to hide the rips and stains in the upholstery.

"Payback! For what?"

"Not cooperating as much as you wanted." He climbed into the truck and yanked the door closed with another protesting screech of metal.

She rapped her gloved knuckles on the window.

He looked as annoyed as she felt, but he rolled down

the window a few inches. His aqua eyes skated over her face. "Now what?"

"If I wanted payback," she said evenly, "I would also write you up for the broken taillight and the expired tags on this heap of rust. Instead, I'll just offer a friendly warning to get them taken care of as soon as possible."

"Or?"

"Or the next patrolman who gets stuck on traffic duty might not be so easygoing about it and you'll end up owing even more money that it doesn't look much like you can afford." She stepped back from the truck and smiled tightly. "Drive safe, now. I don't know what sort of conditions you were used to before coming to Wyoming, but the roads are treacherous in this kind of weather."

His lips thinned. He rolled up his window and cranked the engine. It started after a few tries, belching a cloud of black smoke from the tailpipe.

Ali winced and tucked her nose back into the protection of her knit scarf and watched him drive away.

Chapter Three

"You should have let Cooper skate on the expired parking meter."

Ali set the mineral water and lime and the order of onion rings on the table in front of her sister Greer. If Magic Jax wasn't so busy, she'd have set herself down, too, in the seat opposite her. "I had to choose between citing Grant Cooper or getting skewered by my sergeant again. If Gowler has an actual reason to write me up, it'll be the first nail in my coffin with the department. And he only needs three nails."

"He's not going to fire the only female officer he's got," Greer countered. "Particularly if she's not guilty of anything more serious than letting a new resident off a minor infraction with a warning. Everyone else with the department does it from time to time. Why not you?"

"Everyone else doesn't make the mistake of dating his precious son, Madame Prosecutor. I am not taking any chances."

Greer gave her a look. "I'm a defense lawyer."

"Don't remind me." Greer was the oldest of the three triplets and worked with the public defender's office. Maddie was the middle triplet. The ultimate do-gooder, she was a social worker with family services. Because of her role there, the family court judge had agreed to let her be the temporary caregiver for Layla.

Ali gestured at the stack of files sitting on the table next to her sister's elbow. The public defender's office workload was so huge that they also had a rotating crew of private attorneys who took cases pro bono. "Always trying to get the people I arrest off with just a slap on the wrist."

"You do your job and I'll do mine. That's how it works. Gowler aside, you could have at least bargained a little with Cooper over the ticket. You catch more flies with honey, you know."

Ali didn't dare slip her toes out of her high-heeled shoes so she could wiggle some blood back into them. If she did, she feared she would never get her feet back into the shoes. And she really didn't want to hear Greer's advice at the moment. "You want anything else to go with those onion rings?"

"I shouldn't even be eating these." Greer plucked a ring from the basket. Magic Jax didn't provide a full menu, but they did offer the usual types of bar food. "But I'm starving. Came straight here from the office."

"If you change your mind, let me know." She grabbed her tray and headed back to the bar, picking up empty glasses along the way. It was even busier than it had been the night before. Part of that was because it was Friday night. A larger part, she figured, was because Jax himself was actually mixing drinks behind the bar. For as long as she'd been picking up shifts at Magic Jax, she could only recall a handful of times when he'd actually played bartender.

Every time he did, though, word seemed to spread and the ladies came in droves.

It wasn't surprising. Jaxon Swift was rich. He didn't take any part in the running of the family oil business like Linc did, but he was still part of Swift Oil. He was also as handsome as a blond devil and loved women just as much as they loved him. In short, nothing much had changed since he and Ali had been in high school together.

And now, thanks to Maddie marrying his brother, Linc, they were theoretically one big happy family.

She went behind the bar to rinse the empties and stack them in the dishwasher tray. "Busy night. I didn't expect it to be, considering the snow today," Ali said to her boss.

Jax took the lid off the blender and filled three hurricane glasses with the virulent pink daiquiris that the giggling college girls at table four had ordered. "Busy is the way I like it." He set the glasses on a tray, leaving Ali to top them with the requisite whipped cream and sliced strawberry. He glanced at his next order and reached for a bottle of wine with one hand and a bottle of gin with the other. "Keeps us all in business."

They both glanced toward the door as it opened and a flurry of snowflakes danced inside. A few more women hurried in and started shimmying out of their cold-weather gear. One wore a spaghetti-strapped blue sequin dress under her parka. The other had on a strapless red corset with rhinestone-studded jeans.

Both fluffed their hair as they focused on Jax behind the bar.

Ali had a hard time not rolling her eyes as she finished fanning one of the strawberry slices over a mound of cream. "I think I'm the only one here who's never wanted to date you," she told him.

He chuckled. "What about Greer?"

"Greer never dated anything except her textbooks. Besides, it would have been gross. You went out with Maddie."

He deftly poured two glasses of wine, set them on a tray for Charlene and tossed the empty bottle into the bin beneath the bar top. "Yeah, but she married my big brother." He shrugged and grinned. "No accounting for taste, sometimes." He quickly prepared a gin-and-grapefruit, shaking out the last few drops of grapefruit juice from the plastic pitcher before tossing it into the stainless-steel sink, and added the glass to Charlene's order. "No more grapefruit." Then he picked up a knife and finished prepping the last daiquiri while she fussed with her second one. "You're lagging, Ali."

She rolled her eyes as she picked up the tray and headed around the bar again. After delivering the drinks, she went over to the newcomers, who were still hovering near the entrance. She didn't recognize them. "Help you find a place to sit?"

One of them bit her deeply red lip. "We wanted the bar."

Ali looked over her shoulder. There were a half-dozen bar stools and all were occupied.

By women.

"You're welcome to wait, but I think it might be a while." She gestured at a two-top in the far corner. It, and one other just like it, were the only vacant tables in the place. "If you change your mind, just grab one of those over by the pool table." She barely paused as she spoke, since standing still for too long just reminded her how sore her feet were.

She made the rounds of her tables again and headed back to Jax with a fresh set of orders. Then she went into the small kitchen and dumped another bag of already breaded onion rings into one fryer basket and added similarly prepared chicken fingers to a second.

She left them bubbling merrily away in their vats of hot oil and nipped into the employee bathroom long enough to pee and wash her hands. Then it was back to the fryer, then to the drink station to fill some water glasses, and then out to see if Corset and Spaghetti had decided to forgo the coveted stools at the bar for a table.

They had, and she went to deliver water to them and collect their orders. "First time in?"

Corset nodded and fluffed her hair again. "We drove over from Weaver."

Ali lifted her eyebrows. The thirty-mile drive between Braden and Weaver was tedious even without snowy conditions. "Hope you're planning to spend the night in town. Probably going to be hard getting back there tonight. What can I get you?"

"Do you have a menu?"

Most people didn't bother asking. "Sure." She grabbed one from another table and returned with it. "It's a full bar, so we can make most any drink you want." She smiled. "Unless it takes fresh grapefruit juice. We ran out a few minutes ago." It was obvious to her that they weren't ready to make a decision since they were too busy ogling Jax. "I'll come back in a few minutes and check on you."

She headed back through the tables, only to stop short at the sight of her sergeant coming in. But then she straightened her shoulders. There was no rule against her working a second job, and plenty of the other guys did it to help supplement their public-servant wages. She headed toward him. "Good evening, sir. I'm afraid we've only got one table left—"

Gowler lifted his hand, cutting her off. His usual scowl was in place and he looked no more pleased to be there than she was pleased to see him. "Heard you were moonlighting here these days."

No matter what logic told her, she felt the alarm like a swift, oily wave inside her stomach. "Temporarily."

"Whatever," he said, dismissing her reply. She didn't even have time to draw a breath of relief before he plowed on. "Got a disabled vehicle out on the expressway. Need you to get on some real clothes and report for duty. Get things moving before we've got something worse on our hands."

The "expressway" was Gowler's favored term for the highway between Braden and Weaver. Mostly because it was in no way an express. The road was narrow. Winding. Just two lanes for most of the distance between the sister towns. And unfortunately, it was the site of increasingly frequent accidents. The more Weaver continued to grow—mostly because of people going there to work for Cee-Vid, an electronics and gaming manufacturer—the more people there were traveling back and forth between the sistering towns.

She stifled the "why me?" that hovered in her mind and nodded. She knew if Gowler had had a choice, he'd never have asked her to pull overtime. He hated when the excess pay screwed with his sacred budget. "I just need to let Jax know. He'll have to call in another cocktail waitress."

Gowler waved, looking impatient. But not even his mammoth-sized ego was large enough to think he could order her to do otherwise. Particularly where the Swift family was concerned. Swift Oil was integral to the town's existence. "Do what you've got to do. Then get your rear out to mile post seventeen." He turned on his boot heel and stomped back out the door.

Jax was a lot more understanding than Charlene when Ali broke the news that she had to leave. But then Jax wasn't the one who had to cover all the tables until he found someone else to come in at the last minute on a Friday night.

As she rang up her last set of orders, her gaze fell on Greer. The onion-ring basket was half-empty and she had files spread out all over her table. Greer didn't seem to be aware of anything going on around her as she bent her head over her work. Her dark hair was twisted up in one of her fancy chignons and the only movement she made was with her pen as she scrawled notes on a legal pad.

"Get Greer to fill in for an hour," Ali suggested to Jax.

She left him giving her sister a speculative look and went to the employee bathroom again to change back into the uniform she'd just changed out of only a few hours earlier. She was dog-tired and didn't really look forward to spending any time out on the dark, snowy highway. But there was one bright spot: she got to peel the high-heeled pumps that she had a hate-hate relationship with off her feet.

She rolled up the cocktail uniform and stuffed it in her carryall, pulled on her overcoat and headed out to the front again.

Greer spotted her and gave her the stink eye around Jax as he stood next to her table, clearly trying to talk her into emergency-waitressing for him. Ali smiled broadly as she headed out the exit. Greer would never be able to flat-out refuse their brother-in-law's brother. And in Ali's opinion, her legal-eagle sister could stand an hour or two slinging drinks like common folk.

The traffic was backed up so badly on the highway that it took Ali nearly an hour to work her way through it. She had to weave slowly between cars on both sides of the road with her beacon flashing before she got to the sight of the disabled truck. One of the county deputy sheriffs from Weaver was already on site, but it was obvious that he'd arrived only a few minutes before Ali had.

She grabbed a bright orange vest from her emergency kit and pulled it over her coat as she jogged across the headlight-illuminated road to where he'd set out flares. "Hey, Dave," she greeted when she got close enough to recognize Dave Ruiz. He was a longtime deputy with plenty of experience when it came to their expressway. Far more experience than she had, at any rate. "Miserable night for this particular pleasure, but nice to see you all the same."

Dave, wearing a similar vest, handed her a bundle of flares. "You, too, Ali." He gestured at the semi-trailer that was on its side, blocking both lanes of traffic. "Driver's cleared the debris from the hay bales he lost, but we're still waiting on the tow to get it back on its wheels."

If it hadn't been for the headlights and the glow of the flares, it would have been impossible to see much of anything. As it was, the lights reflecting off the falling snow made their task even harder. "At least this wasn't two miles up the road."

"Amen to that. We'd have had someone go off the curve for sure. All we have to deal with now are a bunch of pissed-off, impatient drivers." The deputy pointed at the toppled trailer. "If we could get some snow cleared away from that side of the trailer, we could redirect traffic one-by-one past the block."

She squinted at the vehicles crowded around them. "Going to have to get each side to give an inch or two."

He grunted. "Yep." He jerked his head. He was wearing a dark beanie, same as she was, and snow clung to it. "Already got a Good Samaritan working on our side to get 'em pulled back some. Busy night with the snowstorm, or we'd have more boots on the ground here."

"Help is help. I'll work on my side," she said. "Considering the angle of the trailer, might be easier if we started letting my side go through first."

"That was my thinking, too."

Happy that they were on the same page, she lit a flare and started working her way back along the highway, dropping the flares as she went to outline the improvised route.

When she was finished, she walked back along the line of bumper-to-bumper vehicles, telling each driver what the plan was and assuring them they were trying to get the road passable as quickly as they could. Her feet were cold again inside her boots, but at least they didn't ache the way they had in the high heels.

There was no room to use the plow on the front of her unit or Ruiz's, so she pulled the snow shovel she always carried from the back, headed over to the end of the long semitrailer and started attacking the berm that had built up from weeks of snowplows clearing the highway. It was a good four feet high, packed hard with ice and snow and dirt, and she was already breathless when someone carrying a pickax joined her.

"Fancy meeting this way."

She went still, peering at the tall figure. "Mr. Cooper?"

He had on a proper coat and gloves at least, though his head was still uncovered.

"Might as well make it Grant, Officer Ali." With a smooth motion, he swung the sharp tip of the pickax into the iced-over mound. "I'll break. You shovel."

It was too much effort to argue, particularly when the idea was a good one, and between the two of them, they managed to break down a car length's worth of snow and ice, shoving the clumps off into the ditch on the other side. The ditch wasn't terribly deep, but it could break an axle if a driver wasn't careful. They both moved farther along the berm and continued.

"You always carry a pickax around with you?"

"Doesn't everyone?"

"Your truck parked somewhere in this logjam?"

"'Bout a mile back on the other side."

"So you are capable of a straight answer." She stopped for a minute to catch her breath and rub the growing ache in the small of her back. She was in good shape, but this was a workout like none she'd had in a while. "Have business in Weaver?"

He, on the other hand, just kept swinging away with the pickax. The guy was like a machine. "My sister isn't in Weaver."

Too proud to let him make her look weak, she jabbed the tip of the shovel into the mess again and resumed pitching it off to the side. "That's not really what I asked."

After siccing Jax on Greer back at the bar, she was going to have to work hard to get her sister to let her use her sweet, claw-foot bathtub back at the house tonight. When she and her sisters had bought the place, they'd agreed to pay separately for the renovations to their own bedrooms and en suite bathrooms, but combine their funds to restore the rest.

A fine idea in theory.

Except that Ali's bathroom was still a work in progress. It had a plywood subfloor perpetually in wait for tile, a sink that worked most of the time and a shower that didn't. Since Maddie had moved in with Linc, Ali had taken to regularly using her shower. But a shower wasn't going to help her aches and pains anywhere near enough after tonight.

Greer, on the other hand, had immediately redone her bedroom and bath. In the entire house, it was the one haven from all that was broken or about to break down. And her claw-foot tub was seriously a thing of beauty.

"It's what you meant," Grant countered.

She didn't bother correcting him, since it was true. "You bought the Carmody place quite a few years ago."

The sharp tip of his pickax sliced cleanly through the snow and ice. "Your point?"

She possessed excellent peripheral vision. Which was handy, because she could watch him without seeming to watch him. "You left it vacant for a long time."

"No law against that." He moved farther along the berm, chipping away faster than she could shovel.

She clenched her teeth and sped up, even though her muscles protested. From behind the truck trailer, she heard engines revving up. Impatient drivers were starting to get a scent of freedom. Just to be safe, she left the shovel standing in the berm and walked back to the first car. The middle-aged driver—smoking his way through a pack of cigarettes if the butts sitting on the road were any indication—rolled down his window when she approached.

Smoke wafted out around her and she coughed once.

A lot of her fellow officers smoked, but she'd never understood the appeal.

She repeated what she'd told him once already. "I'll come back and let you know when it's safe to proceed. It's still gonna be a little while yet, I'm afraid."

He swore. "Little lady, I've got places to be."

She smiled, though she wanted to grind her teeth. "We all do, sir. Might want to consider preserving your gas a little if you can stand the chill—"

He swore again and rolled up the window, cutting her off. He did not turn off his engine.

She straightened, headed back to her shovel and pulled it from the snow. "Just another night in paradise," she muttered.

Already two yards farther than he had been, Grant paused. "Say something?"

He'd done such a good job of breaking up the berm that all she had to do was push the tip of the shovel against the road to plow the chunks off into the ditch. "You're pretty good at this. Had a lot of practice?"

He didn't answer.

"Naturally," she said under her breath.

They chipped and plowed for another few minutes when she saw Dave Ruiz signaling with his mag light.

They'd cleared about thirty feet of iced-over berm.

"That's good enough to start," she told Grant, and his rhythmic swinging immediately ceased. He hooked the deadly tip of his pickax over his shoulder and headed off.

"Thank you," she called after him.

He didn't pause. Didn't look back. Merely lifted his left hand in acknowledgment.

The less he said about anything, the more curious she got.

The feminine side of her wished she wasn't so darn

predictable. The cop side of her just accepted the fact that she was always curious where all people were concerned. Not just enigmatic, aqua-eyed men.

She propped her shovel against an upturned wheel on the trailer as she walked back around it, stomped her feet hard against the road to make sure she still had *some* feeling in them and returned to the first car in the lineup. "I'm going to walk ahead of you until you're past the trailer," she told the driver. It wouldn't speed up the process any, but she wasn't taking any chances on an impatient man going off into the ditch and suing the department as a result.

And one by one, that's how she slowly cleared enough of the road on her side to allow traffic on Dave's side a chance of squeaking around the trailer.

Eventually, she was able to get back into her own SUV, crank up the heater and call in the progress as the traffic slowly crawled along the flare-lined path. About two hours after they'd started, three heavy-duty tow trucks arrived and they had to block off the road again from both sides to allow them space to get the semi back up on its wheels.

The only saving grace was that the snow stopped falling halfway through the mammoth task. But when it did, the temperature dropped another ten degrees and the wind—always pronounced, particularly along this highway cut into the hills—picked up.

But finally, the deed was done. The semi was hitched to the back of another tractor and was headed down the road to Braden. The highway returned to its usual quiet midwinter-night state. Dave and Ali congratulated each other on getting the job done without any collisions or injuries, and they all headed home.

When Ali finally made it there, she noticed Greer's

car parked in her half of the detached garage behind the house. In the kitchen, the slow cooker was sitting on the plywood counter. Stone-cold. Full of uncooked ingredients. Ali had forgotten to turn it on when she'd left the house this morning.

She clamped the lid back on top and left it. It wouldn't be any worse come morning and she could deal with it then.

She dragged herself up the narrow staircase and decided she was too tired to worry about waking up her sister to beg to use her fancy-ass bathroom. Instead, she turned on Maddie's shower and stripped once the bathroom was full of steam.

Then she *finally* stepped beneath the blessedly hot spray. She expected her mind to go blank as she stood there, unmoving, her eyes closed while the water rained down on her head. But she was wrong.

She kept thinking about Grant Cooper. Working beside her. Without being asked. Without complaint. Then just walking away.

She shivered, and realized the water was running cold. She shut it off, stepped out and wrapped a towel around her body. Then she wrapped another towel around her head, returned to her own bedroom, climbing in bed just like that, and pulled her quilt up to her ears.

She wasn't even able to enjoy the grateful thought that she didn't have to work the next day before she was out cold.

Chapter Four

Grant eyed the cardboard box sitting on the front porch.

He hadn't noticed it the night before when he'd finally gotten home after the mess on the highway. The bulb in the porch light fixture still didn't work even though he'd replaced it, and it was a wonder he hadn't tripped over the carton in the dark.

He didn't have to open the box to know what was in it. His publisher's logo was imprinted on the side. The address of his cabin in Oregon was crossed out. The address where he stood now had been marked over it in slashing black ink. Because, God forbid, his author copies of *CCT Final Rules* should have remained behind at the cabin, along with everything else he didn't want.

Just like Officer Ali Templeton, his ex-wife publisher had found him.

He grabbed the box and carried it inside, dumping it on the fireplace hearth.

He'd burn them right now, except he'd probably also end up burning down the entire house. Considering the overall condition of the place, he wasn't setting a match to anything in the fireplace until he got a chance to have the chimney inspected.

He knew he had electrical problems. The porch light was just one example. He also knew he had plumbing problems. The kitchen faucet only worked on hot. The shower in his bathroom upstairs only worked on cold, which meant he was out of luck because the bathtub in the bathroom downstairs was too damn short. He was also pretty sure he smelled something burning every time he turned on the furnace, which was why he wore a damn coat inside the house, even when he was sleeping.

He could make things a lot easier on himself by giving up the notion of living here.

He could go back to Oregon anytime he chose. Calling his place there a "cabin" was basically just a nod to the fact that it was located on a remote, forested ridge that overlooked the wild coastline. But it had plenty of amenities. All the electrical outlets there worked. His shower had eight jets, and they all produced hot water. He could also go to the condo in Los Angeles that had sat vacant for more than a year while he'd holed up in Oregon pulling words out by his teeth to finish writing the book he hadn't planned to write in the first place. And if he really wanted a different flavor, he'd never gotten rid of the New York brownstone that he and Chelsea had shared. When they'd gotten divorced, she'd moved into an apartment closer to her Manhattan office. He'd gone to Los Angeles, putting as much distance as he could between them.

Any one of those properties was by far better than

this run-down ranch house he'd decided to fix up himself. But he had no desire to go anywhere else.

He just wished the box of books hadn't found its way to him. It meant that he'd be hearing from his ex-wife sooner or later. Not because she harbored some emotional leftovers from their marriage, but because she still wouldn't accept his decision to quit writing.

She called it a waste. Accused him of being lazy. Lacking ambition.

His gaze landed on the ancient mirror on the wall. The image looking back at him seemed to smirk.

"Right." He grimaced. "That's what you get for being married to your publisher." He turned away. Nobody stood to make more money on another *CCT Rules* book than Chelsea did.

Not even him.

It was too cold inside the house to paint the walls. Besides, the holes in the plaster that he'd spent the previous evening patching were still damp. The gas stove in the kitchen worked—and he had even installed a couple of the cabinets now—but there was nothing in the refrigerator. That was what had driven him out the front door in the first place when he'd spotted the book shipment.

He went back outside and pulled the door closed behind him. Out of habit, he started to lock it, but didn't. If anyone wanted to break in to steal a couple gallons of paint, they probably needed them more than he did. If they stole the plastic-wrapped couch…well, he could order another one online the same way he had this one.

It had seemed necessary to put at least a few pieces of furniture in the house when he'd gotten here. He might not have unwrapped the couch yet, but he'd been using the mattress set from the first night it had been delivered.

He crossed the cold, hard ground between the house and the barn, following the path he'd shoveled yesterday morning. The snow had nearly filled it up again, but he didn't mind. Shoveling snow was mindless muscle work. Yeah, he had to concentrate harder than he wanted to in order to keep his brain from dwelling on anything other than where to pitch the next shovel of snow, but at least with the physical exertion and then the highway mess, he'd slept more than an hour at a stretch last night.

Instead of nightmares of Afghanistan, his fitful dreams had been about a chocolate-eyed brunette with blond streaks in her hair. And for once, the cold shower had been handy.

He pushed open the oversize, rolling barn door and studied the two vehicles inside. He'd bought the black SUV two months ago. It had every bell and whistle: the car salesman's fantasy sale. And it had gotten Grant from Oregon to Wyoming in perfect comfort.

Instead of heading to the SUV, he went to the rusted pickup. Why not? He'd bought the ranch lock, stock and barrel. That included whatever was left behind on the property. And the truck had definitely been left behind. He'd even found the faded title to it when he'd scrubbed the kitchen enough so that he didn't feel like he was still back in Afghanistan. It had been stuck to the bottom of one of the drawers, along with a newspaper ad for dial-up internet and a half-empty roll of hard candy.

The name on the title was Roger Carmody.

Grant knew Roger Carmody was dead. He had no living heirs. Except Grant, the illegitimate grandson Roger had made certain never used the Carmody name.

Grant had grown up knowing exactly who his biological family was. And he'd known that they didn't want him.

The same perverseness that had made Grant buy the property when it had gone to auction had motivated him to get the hunk of rust running. It was the same perverseness that had him getting behind the wheel and driving the truck now.

"Too bad, Rog," he muttered, cranking the key in the ignition. The engine sputtered a few times, but it started. Grant didn't consider himself a great mechanic, but he figured with enough tinkering, he'd get rid of the sputter, too. The same way he'd get the cold water going in the kitchen and the hot water in the shower. It just took time.

And all he had these days was time.

He drove out of the barn, closed the door behind him and then headed into town. The parking ticket Officer Ali had given him had fallen onto the floorboard on the passenger side and was fluttering in the blast of air from the heater.

It was still fluttering when he parked in front of the town's municipal building. He saw the parking sign and grimaced, checking his pockets for coins.

"There's free parking around the back of the building." An attractive woman bouncing a red-cheeked baby on her hip smiled at him from the sidewalk. Her eyes were friendly. Bright. "They just won't post a sign that says it. Silly if you ask me." She pointed. "Turn at that corner, then make another quick right. You can't miss the parking lot."

He pulled out his keys again. "Thanks."

"You bet." She turned, and her long dark ringlets bounced against the back of her coat as she pulled open the glass door of the municipal building and went inside.

He drove to the corner, made two rights and found a space in the parking lot. Ticket crumpled in his hand, he went into the building from the back. A guard directed him to the cashier's office and he joined the short line in front of the counter. The town wouldn't advertise the free parking in back of the municipal building, but it spared no expense on signs warning the line occupants to remain behind the wide yellow line painted on the floor until it was their turn to approach the cashier. Small-town idiosyncrasies at their best.

The woman with the ringlets and the baby was in front of him. Her eyes crinkled a little as she turned and smiled at him. She was older than he'd first thought. That wild brown hair was deceptive. Then the baby wrapped a hand in her hair and gave a merry yank that had her wincing, even though the smile in her eyes never dimmed.

It felt rude to stand there and not say something, considering her friendly smile. "Got quite a grip there," he said.

"I'll say." She flipped the rest of her hair around her other shoulder, trying to keep it away from the baby. "I ought to have learned by now." She realized the person in front of her had stepped up to the yellow line. Now only she and Grant were still in line. "You know what they're like, though."

He smiled noncommittally. What he knew about babies was somewhere between nothing and less than nothing. Being godfather to Seymour's twins didn't change that. He and Seymour had watched their baptism via Skype. Grant sent Claudia checks on their birthday and at Christmas so she could buy whatever she figured they needed. And unfailingly, within a few days, he received thank-you notes printed in their youthful handwriting.

The line moved forward and he automatically shuffled forward, too.

He never had to wonder what age Eva and Emi were.

They'd been born the same day their father saved Grant's life at Hunt Ridge. Eleven years ago. Covering Grant's body with his own while RPGs and machine-gun fire rained over them because Grant, with his specialized skills, couldn't be as easily replaced as Seymour.

If Grant had stayed in the service, would Seymour still be alive today?

He didn't have the answer to that. Never would.

And it haunted him. Morning. Noon. Night.

"Mom!"

His attention was yanked back to the present. The person working at the cashier's counter was none other than Officer Ali.

And she was looking at the lady in line in front of him. Calling her *Mom*.

"What're you doing here?"

"Paying the water bill." The woman jiggled the baby and pulled an envelope out of her purse as she moved to the counter. "I thought I'd mailed it, but I guess I forgot. What're *you* doing here? You're supposed to be off this weekend."

"Well, clearly, that didn't work out. Gowler called me in again 'cause Jerry's out with the flu." Officer Ali stood up from her chair to reach for the baby, but froze for a second when she spotted Grant standing behind the yellow line.

She wasn't wearing her police uniform or the short, figure-hugging red dress. This time she had on a thick pink sweater, and her hair—instead of being scraped back in a tight knot or flowing in a mass around her shoulders—was pulled back in a messy ponytail.

She was still looking at him, so he inclined his head slightly. "Officer Ali."

Her mother looked back at him with a surprised expression as she surrendered the baby to her daughter. "You know Ali." Her smile was suddenly even wider. "Well, now. Isn't that nice."

He held up the parking ticket between two fingers. "Depends on how you look at it," he said drily.

She chuckled. "Oh, well. Blame Growler. He's positively anal about some things."

"Mom!"

The woman took no notice of her daughter's horrified exclamation. "I'm Meredith. Ali's mother. And you are—?"

In the wrong place at the wrong time. "Grant," he answered.

"You're definitely a new face around here." Meredith's musical laugh fit the sparkle in her bright blue eyes. "And a handsome one, too. Is there a Mrs. Grant?"

"Mom!"

Noting Ali's reddened cheeks, Grant's mood suddenly lightened. "Who's Growler?"

"Gowler," Ali said through her teeth, "and with my luck, he's standing behind the wall, overhearing all of this."

"He's her sergeant," Meredith explained in a loud whisper. "He's been giving her a hard time ever since she dumped his—"

"Muh-ther!" The baby joined the game, too, letting out a loud, garbled squeal that didn't drown out Ali's pained exclamation.

Ali carried the baby around the counter and dumped her in her mother's arms. "Do you need a receipt for the payment?" She didn't wait for an answer. "No? Okay then." She went back behind the counter and looked at Grant without really looking at him. "Next!"

Instead of being upset at her daughter shutting her down, Meredith appeared as if she wanted to laugh more than ever. "Don't let Ali's bark scare you too much. She doesn't really bite."

Pity.

He looked Ali's way, having the good sense to keep the thought to himself. He may have been living like a hermit for the last year, but he still possessed some social sense. "I'll keep that in mind," he told her mother when she carried the baby out of the cashier's office.

Then it was just Officer Ali and him.

He stepped over the yellow line and approached the counter, setting down the crumpled ticket and flattening it beneath his palm. "You look like you need some sleep."

"Flattery won't get you out of the ticket." She tugged it free of his grasp. "I assume you're here to pay the fine?"

He pulled out his wallet. He'd used most of his cash on dinner at the grill in Weaver the night before, so he'd pay with his credit card. "I assume that's true?" he asked, tapping the corner of the card against the laminated Cash or Credit Only sign taped to the counter.

"Yes." She delicately pinched the edge of the credit card between thumb and forefinger as she took it from him and ran it through her machine. "I really would let you out of the fine if I could. You were a big help last night." Her lips suddenly rounded. "Oh," she murmured. She looked up at him. "I'm sorry. Your card was declined."

He frowned. "Try again."

She slid the card through the machine once more, then looked at him a moment later with the same expression. Embarrassment. Sympathy. "Do you have another method of payment?"

He held open his wallet so she could see the meager supply of single bills inside.

"Well—" she held out his card "—don't worry. You still have thirty days to pay the fine." She hesitated for a moment. "If you're looking for work, I can probably recommend a few places—"

"I'll keep it in mind." But he wasn't worried. Irritated? Yes. The card had a massive credit limit. After the money had started rolling in from his first *CCT Rules* book, banks had started throwing credit at him. He'd ignored nearly all the offers. His parents—the ones who *had* cared enough to give him their name after adopting him when he was ten—had been staunchly middle-class. They had passed on their pay-as-you-go mentality to him.

Karen, though, had never seemed to learn the same lesson. She'd just been a baby, already adopted by the Coopers when he'd officially joined the family. She'd never known any other family besides Cal and Talia Cooper. But she'd flown in the face of everything they'd tried to teach their children.

When she'd forged Grant's name on a contract, he'd been glad they hadn't been alive to see it.

He took the credit card back from Ali, making no effort to avoid brushing his fingers against hers, and enjoying more than he should the way she quickly curled them against her palm. But if he expected her dark eyes to shy away from his, he was wrong. "I'll come back with cash." There was a bank not too far away.

"Cashier's office closes at noon on Saturday."

He glanced at his watch. "Then I'll be back before noon."

"Templeton!"

She visibly stiffened and the dark circles under her eyes looked even more pronounced as she stared beyond Grant. He glanced behind him. A uniformed officer stood in the doorway. Except for the paunch he carried, the gray-haired man reminded Grant of one of the drill sergeants from when he'd gone through basic training.

"Yessir?"

"Mendez needs help finding something in the evidence locker."

Her expression didn't change much, but Grant saw the way the skin around her eyes tightened slightly. "I'll get on it."

Grant waited until the officer was gone. "Growler?"

"Gowler. And, yes. He's my sergeant." She set a desk bell on top of the counter, with instructions to ring for assistance, and handed Grant his ticket. She locked a drawer beneath the counter and came out from behind it.

He took in her faded blue jeans and heavy-duty leather work boots.

"Reminds me of a drill sergeant I had a long time ago. He was a royal pain in the ass."

She pressed her lips together, but a faint dimple showed in her pale cheek.

"Every time I see you, you're working one job or another."

"Everyone in the department has to put in their time covering the cashier's office."

"Even Gowler?"

"Theoretically, yes."

Grant lifted his eyebrows and her faint dimple deepened. They headed out into the tiled corridor that led to an information desk in front of a solid door and a long window. A kid sat there, wearing a stiffly pressed police uniform, reading something. He looked so wet-behind-the-ears that Grant was willing to bet it was a children's story. Through the window behind him, Grant could see a half-dozen desks, though only a few were occupied.

Everyone he saw was male, from the kid to the grizzled gray-bearded guy nodding off at another desk behind the window.

"Remember, you've got thirty days to pay the fine."

He'd be back in thirty minutes to pay the fine. "How many women work in the department?"

She looked surprised by the question. "Civilian employees or sworn officers?"

"Sworn."

She shrugged. "Just me."

"And civilian?"

"Darlene Dunworthy—we call her DeeDee—is the chief's secretary."

"That's it?"

"We're a small-town police department. We have fourteen officers and four civilian employees. And not a lot of turnover, so…" She shrugged again. "To use a cliché, it is what it is."

"Templeton!"

She sighed. "I'd better get back to the evidence locker before Sergeant Gowler has a stroke."

"Why's he got it in for you?"

"He doesn't." She made a face. "Well, he does. But he'll get over it. In time." She started to turn away again, only to hesitate. "Do you, ah…lunch? I mean, would you like to have lunch? My treat," she added quickly. "I can't fix the ticket for you, but it seems the least I can do after all the help you gave me last night."

"Or you're trying to sweeten me up to get more information about my sister."

Her eyes narrowed slightly, but the dimple in her cheek didn't go away. "Would it work?"

"We'll never know. I told you that I haven't heard from her in years. There's nothing helpful—"

A phone rang at the information desk, and the kid sitting there startled so badly he knocked his book on the floor. He picked it up and answered the phone.

"—I can tell you," Grant insisted. He lifted his hand. "Scout's honor."

"Were you a Boy Scout?"

"Um, Ali?" the young officer asked, turning red. "Sergeant Gowler says for me to tell you when you're finished flirting, to get your bu—ah, get yourself into his office."

"Great," she muttered, grimacing. "Thanks, Timmy." Then she looked up at Grant. "Sorry."

He was the one who was sorry. Gowler struck him as a jerk, but Grant was the one who'd delayed her.

"Lunch sounds good," he said, moving away from her. "Where?"

Surprise brightened her expression, but it didn't make the dark circles under her eyes disappear. "There's a coffee shop a couple blocks down from here. Josephine's. There's no sign but the name's painted on the front window. North side of the street." She pushed open the solid door next to the window. "My lunch break is at one o'clock."

"One o'clock it is. You can tell me more about Layla."

He hadn't expected to say those words. But he'd said 'em. Maybe the baby was his sister's. Maybe she wasn't. But he knew what it was like being the kid that nobody wanted. "And the foster family she's with."

Timmy—of course, the kid would have a kid's name—looked up from his book. Amazingly, it wasn't a children's book, but had a glossy cover that was way too familiar to Grant. It was a few years old. From when his pseudonym wasn't featured as prominently on the front cover as the title. When there wasn't a photograph of Grant on the back. "Didn't your mom have Layla with her when she came in?" With every word, Timmy's face turned redder.

Ali, though, just looked pained. She let the door to the police department close again.

To her credit, her gaze didn't shy away from Grant's.

"Quite a little detail you left out," he said evenly. He wasn't sure exactly what he felt, knowing that he'd been within touching distance of what was supposedly Karen's baby. "Your mother is fostering Layla?"

"No. My sister is. Mom was babysitting."

"A regular family affair."

"Look, I wasn't trying to hide it. But as you've said, we're only speculating that Dai—that Karen is Layla's mother. Which means you may or may not be the baby's uncle. And her—"

He lifted his hand. "Save it." Through the long window, he could see Gowler stomping around the desks, heading their way.

Her eyebrows drew together. "But—"

"You can explain at lunch."

She nodded quickly. "Yeah. Of course."

The door opened behind her. "Dammit to hell, Templeton! When I say jump, you say how high!"

Grant's jaw felt tight. "She was assisting me."

Pure suspicion filled Gowler's beady eyes, which looked him up and down. "And who are *you*?"

Ali took a step between them. As if to protect him. "This is Grant Cooper," she said quickly. "He's the citizen I told you about who helped us clear the highway last night."

Grant had survived a lot worse than small-town police sergeants puffed up on their own power. Ignoring Gowler was easy. A helluva lot easier than ignoring the odd sensation of having a pint-size police officer trying to protect *him*. "Josephine's at one," he said, then turned and headed back down the hall.

Chapter Five

Ali yanked open the door to the coffee shop and rushed inside. She was thirty minutes late and she half expected Grant to have given up.

But there he sat, in the far booth by the corner window.

Yesterday's snow had given way to clear skies and a winter sun that cast its unforgiving glare across the table. Combined with the sparkling snow outside, it was almost blindingly bright. There were no plates on the table. Just two sturdy white coffee cups, one sitting upside down on a saucer. Grant's long fingers were curled around the other.

Fortunately, she was starting to get used to the jolt she felt whenever she saw him. She figured the reaction would subside soon enough. Pulling off her coat, she crossed the nearly vacant coffee shop and slid onto the padded bench opposite him. "Sorry."

His aqua gaze flicked over her face. "For lying about who has my sister's kid, or for being late?"

She pulled off her scarf and piled it on top of the coat beside her. So much for the niceties. "Then you know your sister had a baby named Layla? You admit she's your niece?"

He spread his fingers. "You tell me, Officer Ali."

She swallowed a sigh. She didn't want to be back at square one with him, but it was her own fault if they were.

"You want more coffee?" She didn't wait for an answer, but slid out of the booth again and went over to the counter. From the pass-through between the kitchen and the front, she could see Josephine working at the grill, so Ali grabbed the coffee carafe from the burner and carried it back to the table. She filled his cup before turning up the second one and splashing coffee into it, too. "You need any cream or sugar?"

He gave her a look. "What do you do? Moonlight here, too?"

"Just habit." She took his nonanswer to mean he liked his coffee black, the same as she did, so she didn't bother to fetch the milk. She returned the carafe to the machine behind the counter and grabbed a basket of fresh rolls before coming back to the booth. "Josephine's rolls are great." She'd been looking forward to them ever since suggesting the coffee shop.

"Have you decided what you want?" She pulled one of the laminated menus from where they stood next to the salt and pepper shakers. "I've had everything on it. Well, everything except the liver and onions. Personally, I can't abide the stuff, but for those who can, it's supposed to be just as good as everything else. Which is very good, I mean." *Good grief, Ali. Just shut your mouth.*

She set down the menu on the table and grabbed her coffee, scalding her tongue when she took too fast a sip.

What was wrong with her? Greer and Maddie may have gotten the brains out of their trio, but Ali had gotten their mother's easy way with people. Old. Young. Female. Male. Okay, particularly male. And she'd never felt tongue-tied around a man. It was just…Grant.

And those damn aqua eyes.

She blew out a breath. "I didn't lie."

He didn't miss a beat. "You didn't present all the facts."

Yep. That was true. No denying it. "Layla is living with my sister Maddie and her husband, Linc."

"Lincoln Swift."

"Yes." She chewed the inside of her cheek. She strongly doubted that Grant would have had a reason to meet Linc, but stranger things did happen. Linc was unquestionably the richest guy in town and Grant was clearly in a different economic bracket—broke, like her. Probably worse than her, because she could use her credit card without it being declined. But none of the triplets had many nickels to rub together, primarily because they'd been feeding all of them into the house they'd bought.

They all loved the Victorian. But it was, unquestionably, a complete money pit.

And yet the wealthy Linc was now married to Ali's social-worker sister. "Do you know him? Lincoln?"

She caught Grant's quick, faint frown. "No."

"You've heard of him, though."

"Swift Oil. Hard not to."

"Right." She nibbled her cheek again. "The house where Layla was left belongs to Linc."

"Thought you said it belonged to Jaxon."

"Well, it does. They're brothers. They both live there. Inherited it from their grandmother. Ernestine Swift. It's a big place." It was Braden's very own mansion that Ali's mother had once cleaned for Ernestine, but that was beside the point.

"Linc's the one who discovered Layla on the doorstep. Jax was out of town. He knew nothing about the baby being left there. Maddie's a social worker and she ended up on the case. Rather than shuffle the baby around in the system, she got the judge to agree to leave the baby in their care while we try to determine exactly what happened." The entire situation hadn't been quite that simple, but that, too, was beside the point. "Except for a few nights, Layla has been with them from the time she was abandoned." The coffee might have scorched her tongue, but the hot cup nevertheless felt good against her palms as she cradled it. She watched him for a moment and wondered what he was thinking, because his eyes weren't giving away a thing.

But they were causing fresh jolts in her stomach whenever he trained his gaze on her.

"You're our closest connection to your sister, Grant. If you're willing, a DNA test would prove a lot. At the very least, whether Karen's just a person of interest, or that she's Layla's mother for certain. It's a simple test, but it would have to be done in Weaver at the hospital."

"No."

She hesitated. "You refuse?" She wondered if her brother, Archer—also an attorney with a good relationship with Judge Stokes—could get the judge to compel the test. Sometimes DNA testing was court-ordered, though it was usually to prove paternity.

"I'm not refusing. I'm just telling you there's no point to it." He suddenly flipped the menu around so that it was facing him. "Both Karen and I were adopted. There's no common DNA to be found between her and me, much less between me and the baby. Who, by the way, looks nothing like Karen. She's got red hair and green eyes. That kid your mother was holding? Blonde and blue-eyed."

Ali felt like the stuffing was leaking right out of her.

She reached for one of the rolls and started shredding it to pieces. "I didn't even consider the possibility you weren't natural siblings," she muttered.

It was no wonder Chief Kessler kept turning down her request to apply for one of the two detective slots in the department. He recognized her lack of investigative ability.

Josephine had come out from the kitchen and stopped next to their table to get their orders. "Hey, Ali. What'll it be today?"

She had been starving, but finding themselves at another dead end where Layla was concerned put a damper on her appetite. "Just the coffee for me, Josephine." She looked at Grant. "You order whatever you want, though. I meant it when I said lunch was my treat."

"Patty melt," he said, setting aside the menu.

Ali nodded her approval. "Good choice."

He looked at Josephine. "She'll have one, too."

She opened her mouth to protest.

"Double fries and two side salads," Grant added. "What kind of salad dressing you want?"

"She likes the vinaigrette," Josephine told him before Ali could voice her objections.

"Make it happen."

"I like him," Josephine said with a wink before heading back to the kitchen.

Ali looked at him. "I'm not hungry."

"Give it a chance. When'd you eat last? I'm betting it was sometime yesterday."

She narrowed her eyes. It had been, but there was no reason he should know that.

"And don't worry. I went to the bank. I've got cash. I paid my parking ticket to young Timmy while you were probably still getting dressed down by your sergeant, and despite the credit-card business, I'm not quite destitute. I can pay for my own lunch."

Considering the state of his truck and his house, she wasn't sure she believed him. But pride was something she definitely understood, having more than a small helping of it herself. "I told you before, it's on me. As a thank-you for your help last night."

"Okay," he finally said. His gaze came to rest on her face. It was just shy of spine-tingling. "Thanks."

Ali actually felt shaky.

He wrapped his hand around his coffee cup again and she moistened her lips, fussing with the coat and scarf on the seat beside her, waiting for the shakiness to pass.

It didn't.

And she decided that maybe she did need some food.

She took a pinch of the shredded roll and sucked it off her fingers.

Across from her, Grant suddenly shifted and his knee bumped hers beneath the table. "Sorry."

She immediately moved her legs to one side to give him more legroom. Josephine's booths had never struck her as too small, but that's how it felt now. She could feel herself blushing and she never blushed. "No worries."

"Why does your sergeant have it in for you, anyway? Is he like that with everyone, or does he just have a problem with female cops?"

"It doesn't have anything to do with anything."

"You like getting picked on then? Just judging from what I saw, the guy's skirting pretty close to harassment. And these days, *that* don't fly."

The conversation was totally slipping off the rails. "He's not harassing me."

"All sorts of harassment, Officer. I'm sure I don't have to tell you that. What's *his* boss think about it?"

"Chief Kessler believes in the chain of command."

"Gowler ride the other officers like he does you?"

She pinched the bridge of her nose for a moment, and then started shredding the second half of her roll. "If I tell you, will you drop it?"

"I guess that depends."

"I can fight my own battles." She couldn't understand why he even cared.

"So you admit it's a battle."

She sighed noisily. "Fine. Gowler was perfectly normal with me—as normal as he ever is, anyway—until I started dating his son. When I stopped dating Keith, the sergeant took it personally." She made a face. "It's silly and going to sound conceited, but he blames me for breaking Keith's heart."

"Did you?"

"*No!* We only saw each other for a few weeks! That's it. We weren't even serious. I mean we never even—" She managed to put a cork in that admission, but Grant's eyes were suddenly glinting.

"At least I wasn't that serious," she said, more or

less evenly. The truth was, she hadn't been *that* involved with anyone for nearly five years. Not since she'd been with Jack. And that was something she definitely wasn't going to share. "But Keith is Gowler's only child. Raised him on his own after Gowler's wife left them when Keith was a baby. Gowler's hard on everyone." She revised that. "Everyone except Keith." The guy was two years younger than her and spoiled as all get out.

"You're making excuses for your sergeant."

"No, I'm just explaining the situation. Sooner or later, Keith will find someone new and Gowler will get over his snit." She made a face. "Admittedly, that snit has been going on for months." A sudden thought occurred to her.

"I think I should be afraid," Grant drawled. "I can see the wheels turning in your head."

She smiled faintly. "Keith's not *all* bad. I mean, I don't think he has a dishonest bone in his body." Unlike Jack. "Even if he *is* a defense lawyer. He just wasn't exactly my cup of tea." She spread her hands, dropping her voice conspiratorially. "But, I could find someone to set him up with. Help him along in his search for his one true love."

Grant gave her a look. "Sounds like a movie-of-the-week plot. And there's no such thing as one true love."

"I don't know about that." She grinned. "And there's a reason why they make those movies. People *like* them. Same way people like shoot-'em-ups and romantic comedies and military thrillers where the good guy whips the bad guy's butt."

Grant waited a beat, then shook his head as if she was more than a little nuts. "And if this unsuspecting female you find also breaks Keith's tender heart? Gowler's not going to blame you for that, too?"

"How could he if he doesn't know I set it up?"

His lips twitched. "I think I'm sorry I asked."

She sat up straighter, feeling restored to her usual keel.

"What's the judge's plan for Layla?"

And...right back into the fire. "Well," she admitted slowly, "that's kind of a sticky area."

"Because—"

"Because, technically, the department's not supposed to discuss details about any minor under protective services except with those who have an official need to know. And there's no actual proof that you're Layla's uncle."

He grimaced. "Damn bureaucracy."

"It's for the child's protection—"

He cut her off. "I get it. Doesn't mean I have to like it."

She started to shift in her seat, remembered his long legs, and stayed put. "I'm not the, um, the official investigator on the case, either." Truth be told, she was lucky that Gowler hadn't barred her from any involvement at all.

"Who is?"

"Detective Draper. He's the senior investigator with the department."

"Can he tell me anything that you can't?"

"No." She pressed her lips together for a moment. "He's been out of the office for a while with the flu." It was Ali, sneaking department resources when Gowler wasn't looking, who'd managed to create a rough map of Grant's sister's movements after she'd quit working for Jax. It was Ali who'd tracked down people who remembered Daisy. She'd worked with them for a few weeks, or crashed on their couch for a few nights. They'd all talked about her nearly obsessive habit of mailing postcards to her sweet Grant.

At first, Ali had thought he was a boyfriend. Lover. Maybe even Layla's father. But the administrator of a shelter in Oregon where Daisy had spent a few nights told Ali that she believed Grant was Daisy's brother.

"Here you go." Josephine returned with their salads and the coffeepot. "You haven't been in here before," she said to Grant as she topped off their cups with steaming brew.

"No, ma'am."

"You look familiar, though."

"I hear that all the time." He shrugged. "Got one of those everyman faces, I guess."

Ali nearly snorted. Everyman? Please.

She waited until Josephine left before she picked up her fork and jabbed at a crisp slice of cucumber. The second she put it in her mouth, her stomach started growling.

Grant clearly heard and his lips twitched. "I knew I was right."

She ignored him and shoveled a forkful of lettuce after the cucumber.

"So." He leisurely shook pepper over his salad. "Tell me hypothetically how this sort of thing works. No names. No specific child. Just the process. What's usually the next step?"

She swallowed. "Well, the judge has some leeway, but ultimately, the goal is to make sure the needs of the child—physical and emotional—are provided for as quickly and as permanently as possible in the best available setting. The child's biological family takes precedence. If one parent is deemed unsuitable, the other parent is looked at. If that parent is unsuitable, then another family member. And so on. Aunts. Uncles. Grandparents and the like, until an appropriate familial setting *can* be found."

"But if you can't establish the identity of at least one of the parents, you can't establish kinship, either."

"Right. In that case—" she spread her hands "—the judge inevitably rules the child be placed for adoption. And he typically decides that within ninety days. Once he rules there is no acceptable parent-child or kinship relationship, he doesn't like leaving that child in the system any longer than he has to."

Grant paused for a moment. "So there's a ticking clock, too."

She nodded. "Look, I'll be honest here, Grant. Assuming your sister *is* Layla's mom, when we find her, she's not going to automatically get back her daughter. She'll be charged with child endangerment. And maybe once that's been dealt with, she'll be able to work with family services to regain some visitation and parental rights. But that's only if we *find* her before the judge has already severed her rights altogether and if Layla hasn't been adopted."

"Layla's a baby." Grant's voice was even. "Everyone wanting to adopt wants a baby. If things get to that point, it'll happen in the blink of an eye."

Had *he* been a baby when he'd been adopted? Considering his troubled expression, she was inclined to think he hadn't been. Which just made her more curious than ever about him.

She focused on her small salad again—a few more bites and it would be gone. Fortunately, she knew from experience that lunch at Josephine's was never a drawn-out affair. The rest of their meal would be coming soon. "Yes, it will happen fast and that's part of the complication." She glanced toward the door when it jingled. An elderly couple entered and took one of the tables in the middle of the room.

She looked back at Grant. "Let's say the child is presently well cared for in a fostering situation. That this situation has been going on for, at a guess, an entire third of the child's life. Then the child is awarded through adoption to a different family altogether. A family who has been waiting on a long list for a long time for just such a child. Much longer than the foster family, who has fallen in love with the child over the past month and whose name is now added to that long list, but at the very bottom of it. The only thing that can slow down this particular train wreck is bringing forward another biological family member."

He considered that for about a nanosecond. "Your sister and her husband still wouldn't end up with her."

"No, but at least we'll all know that we've done everything we can to get Layla to her rightful family. And maybe, at the very least, her new guardian will be open to letting the foster family stay in touch. If it's a traditional adoption, that's not likely to occur. There're lots of reasons to want her with her rightful family." She studied him. "Assuming that her rightful family wants her and can provide a suitable home."

He pushed aside his now empty salad plate. It was perfect timing, because just then Josephine delivered their meals.

Ali studied him. She was still uncertain how he felt—if he would want Layla, should she turn out to be his niece.

Which was something that she now knew couldn't be proven by something as definitive as a DNA test.

They would have to prove it by other means.

And with as little as they had to go on, they might as well be looking for the proverbial needle in the haystack.

"Seems stupid to pull a kid out of the only consistent environment they've ever had."

Ali propped her elbows on the table, leaning toward him over her plate. "You truly have *no* idea where Karen might be?"

He shook his head. His eyes met hers. "If I did, I'd tell you. My sister's always—" He broke off, shaking his head with a sigh. "I don't know. Searching for something she can't ever seem to find."

When he looked at Ali that way, it was like being touched by a live wire. "What about your parents?"

He shook his head again. "Mom had breast cancer. She survived it twice. She didn't make it the third time. And Dad died a few years after her. And to save you asking, no, there aren't any other family members who might still be in touch with Karen. No other family members, period."

"Why do you think she came to Wyoming? There must be some tie for both of you to land here."

"The ranch I bought. I think she was probably staying there without anyone knowing. She was pretty bad about money."

It was a logical enough explanation, though it didn't tell Ali why he'd bought a ranch in Braden in the first place, only to let it sit there vacant for years before deciding to occupy it. "What about her friends? When she was younger? Before you fell out of contact?" She sat forward again. "Where'd you grow up? Maybe I can reach out to former classmates or—"

"Portland, Oregon. She's ten years younger than me. She wasn't the kind of kid who brought home her school friends—at least not when I was still living there. For that matter, she wasn't the kind who went to school all that regularly. But she did graduate high school."

He picked up his sandwich, only to set it back down again without taking a bite. His expression was grim. "I wasn't there to see it. She didn't go to college at all."

Ali couldn't help herself. She reached out her hand and touched his arm briefly. "It's not your fault, you know."

"Don't be so sure. The last time I saw her, I was pretty pissed." For a moment, he seemed like he would say more. But then he merely nodded toward her untouched plate. "Eat."

She picked up her sandwich. "I will if you will."

His faint smile held no amusement. But he picked up his own sandwich and they ate in silence for a few minutes.

Ali knew her allotted lunch break was drawing to a close. But she was reluctant to end it. Not necessarily because she thought she could divine some relevant nugget about Karen, either.

It was all because of him.

"So. What drew you to Wyoming?" She kept her voice deliberately light. "Work or woman?"

He seemed equally glad to lighten the mood. "Both. But *drove* would be more accurate than *drew*."

"Ah." She nodded sagely. "Escaping a sticky situation?"

"Not sticky. Just unacceptable."

"What did she do? Cheat on you?"

At that, he let out a short laugh and all she could do was sit there, feeling bemused. "Nice to see you can laugh."

He shook his head slightly. "Do you always speak what's on your mind?"

She made a face. "If I did, Growler would have fired me by now for sure."

The fine lines beside his eyes crinkled. "Gowler."

"Right." She smiled. "Well, whatever reason drove you to Wyoming, I'm glad you're here now."

"Because of my supposed niece?"

She waited a beat. "Of course."

His aqua gaze lingered on her face and his smile widened. "Of course," he murmured.

She darn near sighed out loud right then and there.

Chapter Six

Grant pulled the truck off to the side of the highway and parked. Then he got out his cell phone and checked the signal. He'd learned all too quickly that the only places where a decent, solid cell signal existed were in the middle of Braden and in the middle of Weaver. Since his house was not in either town, that had been a problem. He wanted away from his old life, but that didn't mean he could avoid everything altogether.

He'd discovered this particular sweet spot on the highway when his phone had rung while he'd been driving.

The sound had been so foreign since he'd come to Wyoming that he'd damn near run off the road. By the time he found the phone—it had slid under the bench seat between an ancient toolbox and a rat's nest of rope—the call had ended and he'd gotten the little *ping* notifying him that he had a voice mail.

Unfortunately, it hadn't been Karen, suddenly reaching out to him after all this time. The message had been from his agent, Martin.

He'd deleted the message without listening to it, pulled back onto the highway and continued driving into town to hit the library for some plumbing books and earn himself a parking ticket.

Now, he sat here on the side of the road while the truck engine rumbled noisily, tapping the cell phone with his thumb and absently noticing the smear of white paint on the back of his hand.

Then he muttered an oath and quickly dialed. It was Sunday afternoon. It would be two hours ahead in New York. But he knew she'd still be at the office, even on a Sunday. Because she was always at the office. That had been part of the problem. She'd worked too much. And he'd cared more about the air force than her.

No wonder they hadn't lasted.

It rang only twice before his ex-wife picked up. "About time you came to your senses," she barked.

"Hello to you, too, Chels."

She made a faint sound that he knew would be accompanied by a roll of her blue eyes. She'd be pushing back in her expensive-as-hell chair, putting her bare feet on the corner of her expensive-as-hell desk and tugging the expensive-as-hell glasses off her face to dangle them at her side. "Hello, Grant," she finally said. "Where are you? Are you calling me from Nowheresville, USA? You didn't have to bug out of the cabin just because the Rules Rabble had started camping outside your door, you know. All you needed to do was hire a decent security team! And to move without even telling me? Or Martin? You know he's been trying to reach you."

The day that he'd met Ali hovered in his mind. When

he heard her pounding on his door, he'd automatically thought she was just another of the rabid fans who'd invaded his remote Oregon retreat to such a degree that he'd taken the drastic action of escaping to a small Wyoming town where nobody would expect to find him. The only person he'd notified about his move had been Claudia Reid. "Martin doesn't have anything to tell me that I want to hear. And it's obviously not Nowheresville here or you wouldn't have been able to get that box of books to me when it was returned to you. You shouldn't have bothered. Waste of postage."

She snorted softly. "I'm your publisher, darling. I have a contractual obligation to get those copies to you."

She'd been his wife before she'd been his publisher. That particular promotion hadn't come about until after their divorce and his second book. "Don't make me tell you what you can do with your contractual obligation." They both knew good and well that the contract she cared about most was for the next *CCT Rules* installment. The contract he refused to even discuss.

She laughed lightly. "Always the same, dear Grant. I would never put up with you if you weren't such a gifted writer."

He wasn't gifted. After getting out of the air force, he'd written the first *CCT Rules* because it had been cheaper penning the stories that kept him from sleeping at night than paying for counseling. Their marriage might have been crumbling, but that hadn't stopped Chelsea from deciding the handwritten scrawls were worth something. She'd nagged him into putting it in actual story form and then ran it past the editorial team where she worked.

Within months, he had an agent, a book deal and a wife who wanted a divorce. Despite that, she was more responsible for the success of the series than he was. She'd certainly benefited from it more than she'd ever benefited from being married to him. His unexpected catapult up the bestseller list, as the first book was followed by another, and another, had been accompanied by her even more meteoric progress up the ranks at work.

"I'm not calling to talk about *CCT Rules*."

"Pity, when it's the only thing at all that interests me."

"Ever honest, even when it hurts, right, Chels?" It was too easy to fall into nasty old habits. "Have you heard anything from Karen lately?"

"Aside from the occasional piece of mail that ends up getting forwarded from wherever? No. I haven't." Fortunately, the sarcasm left her voice.

Once the gloss of "opposites attract" had worn off, Chelsea had been a witch of a wife. To be fair, he hadn't been much of a husband. But for reasons Grant had never understood, his ex-wife had always had a soft spot for his sister.

"I hope you're not lying to me, Chels. This is important."

"Oh, for God's sake, Grant," she snapped. "Have *I ever* lied to you?"

True. They'd been married for seven years. She'd told him everything that was good and everything that was bad. In excruciating detail. She'd often said that she had a closer relationship with her battery-operated boyfriend than she did with him. And, in the end, that it was preferable to him altogether.

"Just tell me what's happened," she said impatiently.

"Nothing good. When's the last time you *did* talk to her?"

"I didn't actually speak with her, because I was traveling, but when I got back from the Frankfurt Book Fair last October, my assistant told me that she'd called. She didn't leave a number or any particular message, but you know Karen. She rarely does."

"Any hint at all where she was calling from? Like a city? A state?"

"No idea. I did send her some money about six months ago, though."

"Chels—"

"Don't even think about lecturing me. I could always tell whether or not she was sober, and she was. She'd met some guy but it hadn't worked out—"

"Because it never works out."

"And she needed to get out of the situation. So I wired some money to her in Montana. Butte. But given her restlessness, I doubt she was still there when she called me again last October."

It was still more information than he'd had. Maybe the situation his sister had alluded to was her pregnancy. "She happen to say what Butte boy's name was?"

"No, but she gave me the address where she was crashing. I needed it for the wire. I'm sure I've got it somewhere. I'll email it to you."

"I haven't checked my email for months. I don't even have a computer with me here."

She clucked her tongue. "You're taking this no-more-writing thing a little too far, don't you think? If you're holding out for more money for the fifth book—"

"I'm not writing a fifth one, Chelsea. I've told you that a dozen times. I'm done."

She sighed again, even more noisily. "You'll change your mind and sign another contract, just like you changed your mind and signed the last one. The money's just too damn good. We've got momentum on our side, Grant.

You don't want to lose that. The usual networks have been clamoring for interviews…"

He hadn't changed his mind about the last one. Karen's forgery of his signature had. And if Chelsea hadn't enlisted Karen's help to convince Grant to sign by luring her with a shopping spree, Karen wouldn't have cared less about the contract. As much as he wanted to blame Chelsea, though, he blamed himself more. He should have been a better big brother when Karen had been growing up. A person couldn't set an example in someone's life if they just weren't there. He hadn't been there for her when Talia died. And two years later, when Cal followed, instead of leaving the air force when he'd had the opportunity, Grant had just re-upped.

He'd been more concerned with trying to prove he was a real chip off Cal Cooper's block than he'd been with taking care of his wild-child sister.

"No interviews."

"But—"

"I said no, Chelsea. You've got the book. That's all you need."

"You know, for a hard-ass air-force hero, you've turned into quite the prima donna."

"I wasn't a hero," he said flatly. "Text me that address. And if you do hear from her, find out where she is. Or tell her to call me."

"Do I get to know why?"

"Because I think she had a baby and she left her on the doorstep of a stranger, rather than reach out to me for help."

"What?"

"Just text me that address in Montana." Before Chelsea could say anything else, he ended the call.

Then he rubbed his forehead, where the headache always formed when he spoke with his ex-wife.

Prima donna.

Hardly.

But he had no intention of telling her the truth. It wasn't that he didn't *want* to write another *CCT Rules*. He was afraid he *couldn't* write another. For one simple reason.

He had no more words left inside him.

They'd died the same day Seymour had.

"You need to get a phone line," Ali said the next morning when Grant opened his front door to find her once again standing on the porch.

He squinted. The sky was still clear overhead and the sunlight was sharp, particularly after a night spent inside a bottle. "What for?"

"So a person can reach you. Obviously." She gave him a knowing look and, without waiting for an invitation, brushed past him to come inside. "A straight-forward telephone line isn't too expensive," she said. "As long as you don't get any bells and whistles—like voice mail, caller ID. That sort of thing. Everyone around here has landlines. Pretty much have to."

Her hair was up in that god-awful knot, but she wasn't wearing her uniform, which he assumed meant she wasn't on duty. Either she recently had been or would be soon. She was wearing jeans and a puffy red coat that ended just shy enough of her hips that a man— if he was looking—could seriously appreciate the glory of her jean-clad butt.

He told himself not to look. And, of course, he did.

He fastened a few of the buttons on the shirt he'd

yanked on when she'd started pounding on his door. "What're you doing here, Officer?"

"Lord, it's hot in here. How do you stand it?" She peeled out of her coat and dropped it on the couch. The thermal shirt she wore hugged her lithe torso like a lover. And he'd have bet his left hand that there wasn't a thing separating her skin from that clinging gray waffle weave.

"Yeah, well, two days ago, it was freezing in here. If I have to pick a poison, I'll take the hot. Now, what—"

"I got a hit on the missing persons." She lifted her hand, forestalling him. "A woman named Karen Cooper was picked up last night during a drug raid in Seattle. She answers the general description—" Ali broke off when he shook his head.

"It's not her."

"Well—" she spread her palms "—have you turned psychic or do you have information I don't?"

"She's not into drugs. That's not Karen's thing at all. She likes to drink."

"Looks to me like she's not the only one," she murmured, picking up the empty bottle of Jack Daniel's lying on the floor next to the couch he'd finally gotten around to unwrapping. She watched him steadily with her big brown eyes. "Pardon me, but weren't you the one to tell me it's been nearly three years since you last had any contact with her? I'm sure you know that a *lot* can happen in three years." Again without invitation, she went into his kitchen, taking the bottle with her.

A lot could happen in three days. Or five. Which was how many days it had been since Ali had knocked her way into his life.

It seemed longer.

"Wow. Fast work. Did you put in the cupboards yourself?"

He joined her just in time to see her drop the bottle in the trash can under the sink. The work had only been fast because he wasn't sleeping more than a couple hours at a stretch and that left a lot of hours on the clock to fill.

"Yeah."

"Nice." She ran her hand over the butcher-block countertop he'd also added. She smiled. "If you ever get bored, I know the owners of a Victorian who need some real help."

He would have returned her smile if his head wasn't ready to explode. "Karen wouldn't pick up drugs."

"Like she wouldn't leave her baby on someone's doorstep? In the middle of winter? With just a note?"

Point taken.

He pulled out one of the chairs at the table and winced when it screeched against the floor. He sat and scrubbed his hands down his face, pressing the heels of his palms into his eye sockets. "Seattle."

"Mmm-hmm."

He heard her moving around and dropped his hands to see that she'd pulled a can of coffee out of the pantry cupboard. "That can is probably twenty years old."

She peeled off the plastic top and showed it to him. "Never been opened. And it's—" she rolled the can in her hands, looking at the label "—only a couple years old." She looked around. "And I don't exactly see a coffeemaker or coffee pods sitting around anywhere."

He got up and pulled a jar off the top of the fridge. He set it beside her. "Because I've been using instant."

"Instant!" She looked from the jar to him.

"Don't give me that look. It's not a ticket-worthy offense. I get the real stuff when I drive into Weaver." As the crow flew, the ranch was closer to Braden than it was to Weaver. But it took less time to drive to the smaller town than it did to get into Braden. "There's a diner there I like. Great coffee. Great rolls. They remind me of the ones my mom used to make."

She nodded. "Gotta be talking about Ruby's."

"You know it, then."

She smiled wryly and continued opening his cupboards and drawers as if she belonged there. She wouldn't find much. They were more empty than not. What they did contain he'd either found stored in one of the boxes in the barn, or he'd purchased at Shop World in Weaver. "I was born and raised in Braden. I know every nook and cranny in this town and in Weaver." She paused, then pulled an ivory card out of a drawer along with a cheap metal spoon. "This important?"

It was the invitation from Claudia Reid.

He shook his head and Ali shrugged, then set it on the counter before picking right back up where she'd left off. "Used to be what one town didn't possess, the other usually did. Now, Weaver's been growing so much what with Cee-Vid's plant being there, that it's going to be bigger than Braden before long."

"Cee-Vid." He reached out and yanked the cord on the metal blinds hanging in the window over the table until they lowered, sort of. Half of the narrow slats were bent out of shape, and no amount of tugging on the cord got the blinds to hang evenly. He gave up and sat back in his seat. "That's the video gaming deal?" He'd driven by the large complex on the edge of Weaver. "Weird place for the company to be located if you ask me. Not exactly Tech Valley here."

"Cee-Vid makes more than just video games." She gave him a look. "They always have a job opening or two." She waited a beat as if expecting a response, but continued when he gave none. "And the company's located in Weaver because the founder is from Weaver. His son—who just so happens to be one of my cousins—is married to the lady who owns Ruby's." She'd found one of the barn-rescued saucepans and started filling it with water. "But the diner's been there since before I was born. People drive from all over to get Tabby's sticky cinnamon rolls, just like they do to get Josephine's liver and onions." She turned off the water and set the pan on the stove, cranking up the flame beneath it.

Then she turned to face him, leaned against the stove and folded her arms. "The clerk I talked to in Seattle is going to send me the mug shot when Karen's through processing. I didn't get it by the time my shift ended or I'd have printed it and brought it out here with me."

He looked at the cat clock on the wall. "It's nine in the morning."

"I worked graveyard last night."

"How long have you been with the department?"

She looked surprised by the question. "Almost ten years. And before you say anything, I know. I should be a detective by now."

He raised his hands in surrender. "I wasn't going to say anything."

"You were thinking it, though."

He gave her a long look. "Trust me, Officer Ali. You don't want to know what I'm thinking."

She shifted suddenly, turning to jiggle the handle of the pan, as if that would somehow make the water heat faster.

His eyes drifted from the dark strands of hair that had broken free from the knot and rested against the pale skin of her neck, down the length of her spine to her backside.

He'd rather think about anything besides Karen. Or Chelsea. But there was a baby to think about who hadn't asked for any of this. "My ex-wife told me she wired money to Karen about six months ago. She was in Montana. I've got the phone number where she was staying." He'd waited for an hour out at that sweet spot on the highway before the *ping* of Chelsea's text message had come through. Had he not hung up on her first, he figured she wouldn't have waited all that time just to tell him that she was still looking for the address. "If she finds the address, she'll let me know."

"That's great!" Ali turned off the flame and took a clean spoon and mug out of the drainer that he'd bought at Shop World. "Even with just a phone number, we can look into it. If it's not Karen in Seattle—"

"It won't be." Despite everything, he refused to think otherwise. "Spoon the coffee into the cup first. Then add the water. Dissolves better." He got up and retrieved the pencil stub and the notepad he'd been using to keep lists of all the crap that needed repair and wrote out the phone number on the bottom of a sheet and tore it off.

"You're quite the instant-coffee aficionado." She twisted off the lid of the jar and spooned a measure into one of the mugs. "Look about right?"

"Little more." He gave her the slip and went back to sit at the table.

She didn't even glance at the number before sliding it into the back pocket of her jeans. Then she tipped some more of the grounds into the cup. "Teach you the fine art of instant-coffee making in cooking school?"

"Afghanistan." He shrugged when her gaze flew to his. "Air force."

"Is that why you fell out of contact with—"

"No."

She waited, her gaze steady.

"I got out nearly six years ago."

"Were you a pilot?"

"Combat controller."

"First There," she murmured. He saw the way her gaze slid to the ivory card sitting on the counter. The lettering was black and somber. At the top, there was a cross with an eagle over the center and the words *For Valor* printed on a scroll beneath it. "I'll bet you have some stories to tell."

He wasn't touching that with a ten-foot pole.

There was no secret that First There was the CCT motto. But in his experience, it wasn't exactly common vernacular for an ordinary citizen. For that matter, most people didn't even know what a combat controller was. "Your daddy serve? Brother?" He waited a beat. "Boyfriend?"

She shook her head, then immediately backpedaled. "Well, my dad was US Army. But that was a long time ago. And my brother, Archer, was never interested. He was too busy becoming Clarence Darrow." She set down the jar and picked up the pan, pouring water into the mug and then stirring it.

"He's a lawyer?"

She handed him the mug, nodding. "So's Greer. She's with the public defender's office. He's in private practice. Has offices here and Colorado."

"And Maddie's a social worker."

She'd started opening cupboards again, and soon found the jumble of old mugs and new plastic cups. "With a highfalutin psychology degree. Not quite as highfalutin as Hayley's, but close." She managed to extract a mug without sending the whole mess tumbling.

"Hayley's—"

"My oldest sister. Half sister, actually. She's a psychologist. Has a practice in Weaver." Ali didn't bother using the spoon to scoop grounds into the cup this time, just poured straight from the jar. "There's Arch, then Hayley, then Greer and Maddie and me."

"The triplets."

She lifted her eyebrows slightly, but didn't question how he knew that. "Hayley and Arch had a different mom," she went on as if he hadn't said a word. "She died before my dad met my mom."

Meredith. The woman with the wild hair and the blonde baby on her hip.

The baby that could be his niece.

He didn't want to think about that, either.

"And you're the cop," he said.

She focused on pouring water over the grounds and nodded. "Right." Then she stirred the coffee and lifted it to her mouth. "Hmm. Better than the stuff we have at the department, but that's all I'll say about it."

"It's hot and it's caffeine. That's enough for me." He'd had plenty of days when his only java came out of his MRE. He pushed one of the other chairs out with his foot and she sat. "How do you know about CCT?"

"I wanted to enlist out of high school." She grimaced. "Both my parents nearly had strokes. We struck a bargain, though. I had to put in two years of college and if I still wanted to go after that, they wouldn't try to stop me."

"Two years was enough to change your mind."

"Well, I still would have gone." She finally lifted her gaze to his. "College was so *not* my thing. But by then, the BPD was making a concerted effort to add some women to their ranks and by some miracle, I got in. My parents still weren't thrilled, but at least I was sticking close to home." She sipped the coffee again, narrowing her eyes against what he himself had already discovered was its blistering heat. "Now, I can't imagine being anywhere else."

"Itchy feet gone?"

"Totally. Braden may be small and pretty simple, but there's no place else on this earth I want to be."

"Doesn't seem like the department did a great job finding many female officers, though."

"There've been a few others over the years. But nobody local. Nobody who wanted to stay. Sheriff's department has the same problem. Both organizations actively recruit woman, but—" She shook her head, shrugging. "Unfortunately, it gives the impression that neither is an equal opportunity outfit."

She propped her elbows on the table, cupping the mug between her hands. "How about you? Don't have much in the way of airports around here needing an air-traffic controller." She studied him. "And for some reason you don't strike me as a natural-born rancher."

Combat controllers were certified FAA air-traffic controllers. They just generally did their work in downright crummy environments, rather than from a well-equipped airport control tower. They were more than just comm specialists. More than weapons specialists and more than demo. They were the air-to-ground liaisons, establishing assault zones and airfields, calling in air strikes and controlling flights, targeting IEDs and manning artillery pieces, and doing it ahead of everyone else so they could do *their* jobs. In Grant's case, he'd done it alongside Seymour's Special Forces unit. If Sey wasn't watching Grant's back, then Grant was watching Sey's.

And now Seymour was dead.

"I know you bought this place nearly a decade ago." Ali's voice drew him out of his thoughts. It was easier facing the frank curiosity in her eyes than it was to think about Seymour. "But as far as I can tell, you didn't do a single thing with the property. Why did you buy it in the first place? We're a long way away to get noticed by a Portland boy. And I get you were on deployment, but you just said you got out several years ago. So why are you only moving here now?"

He hadn't been a *boy* in a long damn time. "You're full of questions."

"And yet you're not real full of answers. Did you get a settlement from your military service or something? Independently wealthy?" She gestured at the cabinets. "You told me you weren't quite destitute, but stuff like this costs money and as far as I can tell, you don't seem to have a source for any."

"Maybe I charged it all on my credit card that wouldn't work the other day."

"Did you?"

It should have been easy enough to just tell her about *CCT Rules*. But he couldn't make himself do it. Because if he did, he knew everything would change.

He didn't want her to start looking at him differently. Expecting him to be the so-called hero the bio on his book jackets described when he knew he was anything but.

So he said nothing at all. "I'm not a suspect in any crime, am I?"

She raised her eyebrows slightly. "Of course not."

"Then a man's got a right to his privacy, Officer Ali."

"Very true, Mr. Cooper." But the expression in her eyes was openly speculative. With her compact little body and her dark, dark eyes, she was nothing at all like the usual women he went for. They were tall Nordic types, both before Chelsea—who'd fit that description to a T—and after her.

Now, here was this short, skinny, nosy cop with a spectacular butt and shining brown eyes. And he was pretty sure he'd never been more attracted to a woman.

He exhaled roughly. "You're right. I'm not a rancher. I'm a—" *Writer who can't write.*

Her eyebrows rose a little more, disappearing beneath the messy bangs. "Yes?"

He drained the bitter, searing coffee. "A guy who bought up a ranch." He was definitely not a hero, couldn't even tell the truth when he wanted. "It was cheap. And it used to be owned by my grandparents."

Chapter Seven

His grandparents?

Ali studied Grant's closed expression. "The Carmodys were your grandparents?"

"My natural grandparents," he said, as if that explained everything. Considering the discontented twist of his handsome lips, though, she had the feeling that there was a lot more to his story.

And while she was intensely intrigued, there was still the pressing matter of Layla. The baby's welfare had to take precedence. Ali had been so excited to share the news about the hit in Seattle, that she hadn't thought much beyond getting here and telling him. Now that she'd done so, what was next?

"Would you be able to come by the department so you can ID the Karen from Seattle to see if it's your sister?"

"She won't be." He pushed to his feet. "But I'll come

just to prove I'm right." He went to the narrow stairs on the far side of the refrigerator and started climbing. "I need a shower first."

She did *not* need the mental image that announcement conjured. "I, uh—" She had to actually clear a knot in her throat. "Do you want me to wait for you?"

"Unless you're gonna come and join me."

She froze, feeling more than a little like a deer in the headlights when he angled his head so he could see her from his vantage point halfway up the stairs.

"No?" His voice was easy as he straightened and continued up the steps. "Too bad," he said over his shoulder. "Shower's hot water doesn't work. Might've made that a little more bearable."

He'd reached the top of the stairs and she could hear the creak of floorboards overhead as he walked.

She exhaled and her head flopped back weakly against the yellow vinyl padded chair. Obviously, he hadn't been serious, but that didn't stop her imagination from going berserk.

A moment later, she heard the rattle and squeal of water running in the pipes. They sounded even worse than the pipes at her place.

It was too easy imagining him stripping off the blue jeans and the plaid shirt, which had two little buttons that had done nothing—absolutely *nothing*—to hide the magnificent torso beneath. He was obviously tall, and he'd struck her as maybe even a little skinny. And here it turned out he had more muscles and ridges running down his chest than Carter had pills.

She exhaled and wiped the perspiration from her forehead. It was almost as hot in his house as it had been at their Victorian before Christmas, when the furnace had been running amok. Their father had finally dismantled the thing, and then they'd gone from wearing shorts and bikini tops to three layers of clothes just to keep warm.

They had a new furnace now, though.

Which was just one of the reasons why Ali still didn't have the money to fix her pickup's transmission.

The pipes were still rattling but she stood and started up the stairs. At the top, there was a closet door in one direction and a short hallway in the other. She passed the first open door—a room that had nothing in it except a stack of yellowing newspapers—and stopped at the second door. She knocked. "Hey."

The running water stopped. "Yeah?"

She smiled a little, inordinately pleased by the caution in his tone. *Not so cocky after all, are you?* "My father replaced our furnace for us last month. I could talk to him. He's retired and he's always looking for—"

The door suddenly opened and Grant stood there, holding a threadbare white towel at his hip.

The water *was* cold. She could see it in the gooseflesh rippling over his sinewy arms. In the tight nipples on his mind-blowing chest. Droplets were sliding down the dark line of hair, bisecting his ribs, collecting in the indent of his navel—

She snapped her eyes back up where they belonged.

But that meant seeing the devilish amusement in his aqua eyes. "Looking for something?"

"Projects," she blurted, feeling hotter than ever. "Sorry." Didn't matter that she was acting like a virginal schoolgirl. She turned on her heel to get the heck out of Dodge.

His hand grabbed her arm from behind, pulling her to a standstill. "Hold on there."

She didn't know what on earth possessed her. She

caught him in a wristlock and the next thing she knew, she'd flipped him to the ground.

"Jesus H. Christ!" He stared up at her, confounded.

Horrified, she quickly let go of him and backed away, only to bump her head against the wall of the narrow hallway. The towel had entirely gone by the wayside and looking away seemed as impossible as jumping to the moon. Or pretending that she hadn't just lost her marbles entirely.

"I'm sorry," she said, hurriedly crouching down to grab the towel and toss it at him. It did not hit the intended target area, but landed in a ball on his belly.

He jackknifed up, clutching the towel in his big hand in front of him as he stood, but it was a case of way too little and way too late.

She wasn't going to be able to close her eyes anytime soon without seeing him in all his masculine glory on the back of her eyelids.

"What the hell, Ali! I wasn't gonna hurt you."

"I know, I know!" She dragged her fingers through her hair and half the pins in her bun scattered. She scrambled to pick them up, and that only brought her closer to the target she was trying to avoid.

Him.

She quickly decided the bobby pins simply weren't that important. "I just, you just…make me jumpy, okay?"

He muttered an oath, raking his fingers through the wet hair hanging in his face.

He was standing in her path to the staircase and unless he turned himself sideways, there was no way she could slip past without brushing against him.

And *that* wasn't going to happen anymore than she

was going to pick up those two pins right next to the big toe on his right foot.

She backed up a step and hit the damn wall again, this time cracking her elbow. "This place is more treacherous than my house!" She rubbed her elbow.

"Yeah, well, you shouldn't go walking around in strange men's—"

"Hallways?"

His eyes met hers. And they suddenly crinkled. He let out a laugh and shook his head. "Damn," he muttered. "This is a first for me."

Her cheeks were on fire, but she felt a smile tug at her lips, too. "Yeah, well, me, too. I've never actually done that. You know. Outside of practice sparring."

"Yeah, well," he returned. He wiggled his wrist. "Nice job. I think."

She bit the inside of her cheek and dragged her eyes upward again. "You, uh, need to, um, adjust your towel or something."

He cursed and she could have sworn his cheeks actually turned dusky.

"I'm just gonna turn around." She spun on her heel until she was no longer facing him.

"Think that's closing the barn door too late, but okay." She felt more than heard him move. "All right," he said a moment later. "You're safe. All clear."

Her chest hurt from the way her heart was thumping so hard. She cautiously turned.

He'd pulled on a terry-cloth robe.

Not unusual, she supposed.

Except this one was bright red. And it had big white hearts splashed all over it.

"Well," she said after the shock of it passed. "I guess you're set for Valentine's Day."

He spread his palms. The sleeves were at least six inches too short on his long arms. "Someone left it in the closet."

"Maybe your sister when she was squatting here without permission." Ali felt confident it hadn't been left behind by the weed-toking teenagers. "Aside from the fact that it's a little short—" A *little*? She could see nearly every inch of his muscular thighs. "—it's a good color on you."

He cupped the edge of fabric where it crossed over his chest. "You're sure it's not too much? I think it's a little bright, but—"

She rolled her eyes.

He chuckled. Made a point of turning sideways and sweeping his arm out in invitation toward the stairs.

She quickly scooted past him. And it was a wonder she didn't fall over her feet, she skipped down the steps so fast.

"I'm gonna wait in my truck," she yelled over her shoulder as she grabbed her coat and kept right on going until she burst out the front door.

She slammed it behind her and stood on the front porch, hauling in the cold morning air. She was so hot—from the furnace, from embarrassment, from *oh, dear God, he had a perfect body*, that she didn't even bother pulling on her coat once she left the porch to climb up into the SUV.

Then she thumped her head against the headrest. "Alicia, you big dummy."

She turned on the ignition and rolled down the window, because she was *still* too hot.

Only a few minutes passed, though, before the front door opened and Grant came out. And she couldn't help but laugh silently.

He'd changed into jeans. And a brilliant red sweater. He, too, didn't seem to feel the need for a jacket. But he was carrying one bunched in his hand.

He jogged across to the SUV. His hair was still wet and slicked away from his angular face. "I'll follow you into town," he said.

"Are you sure?" She pulled her shoulder belt across her lap and fastened it. She grinned. "You can sit up here with me if being behind the grill is too unnerving." The "grill" was a thick web of metal separating the front seat from the back.

His eyes glinted. "I've ridden in the back of scarier cop cars than this," he assured her. "But if I ride with you into town, you're gonna have to bring me all the way back. No point in making a wasted trip."

She held her grin in place, even though it suddenly felt like it had deflated. "All right then," she agreed, in what she hoped was a creditably easy tone. "I'll see you at the department. I'm sure the mug shot will be there by now." She'd radio ahead just to make sure of it.

"Good enough." He tapped the hood of the SUV as he headed toward the barn. He pushed open the door and disappeared inside and a moment later, the rusted pickup truck was coughing its way through the barn door opening.

Once he was through, he got back out, closed the barn door, climbed back in the truck and sketched a wave toward her as he did.

She pulled the SUV around to head back to Braden.

As soon as she reached the highway, she thumbed the radio. "Timmy, did that fax come in from Seattle that I was waiting for?"

Static greeted her. Then an eventual affirmative.

"On my way." She dropped the mic on the console. Grant's pickup truck was in her rearview mirror.

Nineteen-point-six miles to go, and they'd know whether or not Seattle's Karen was their Karen.

She wasn't.

Dismayed, Ali looked from Grant's face to the fax image. The quality of the picture wasn't great, but it was full color. "Are you sure? I know she's a green-eyed redhead, but ignore the brown hair. Contact lenses these days can make anyone's eyes blue like that." For all she knew *his* aqua beams were a result of contacts.

"It's not her," he said again. "I'd know my own sister's face, Ali."

She sighed. "Of course you would." She dropped the fax onto her desk and led the way out the department's security door.

"See you tomorrow, Timmy," she said as they passed the information desk.

He was their newest recruit, and tended to blush anytime she addressed him. Today was no exception. He nodded, red-faced and Adam's apple bobbing. "See ya, Ali."

"Gonna have a hard time as a police officer if he looks like a beet every time he speaks to a woman," Grant commented once they'd left the building through the rear door.

"He's twenty years old. He'll get over it," she said with more confidence than she felt. "I used to be his babysitter. I think maybe he had a little crush on me back then."

"Back *then*?"

"Well, don't go saying anything too loud about it,"

Ali said. "God knows that Gowler would blame me for that, too."

"Didn't notice him strutting around today."

"He's off."

"Will the mice play?"

"Probably." She grabbed her purse from the SUV and relocked the vehicle. "Mind giving *me* a ride home? I'm off for an entire twenty-four hours. Gowler'll be back in twelve. He won't like it if my ride is parked in front of my house instead of here at the department."

"You don't have a car?"

"Bad transmission. Still in the shop. And it's a pickup." They'd reached *his* pickup and she pulled open the passenger door. It squealed as if it hadn't been opened in a decade. Considering the truck had to be at least twenty years old, she figured that was definitely possible.

He got in beside her and the blanket-covered bench seat seemed to shrink. She started to roll down the window for fresh air, but the handle came right off in her hand. "Uh-oh." She held it up for him to see.

"Yeah, it doesn't work." His fingers brushed hers as he took it from her and tossed it over the back of the seat. Since there was no rear seat, it didn't have far to go and she heard it clang against something when it landed. "Don't worry about it."

She rested her bare knuckles against the window. For some reason the cold sensation seemed to make the interior feel a little less confining.

You don't feel confined. You just can't stop thinking about him being naked.

She chewed the inside of her cheek and trained her attention out the windshield.

He drove out from behind the municipal building to the main street. "Which way?"

She scrabbled her senses together. "Left. Then left again at the light. After that it's just basically up the hill."

The street traffic was light. He turned left with ease and drove down the block. Past the central business district and the bus depot; past the Suds-n-Grill and China Palace. She pointed her thumb at the Chinese restaurant when they stopped at the red traffic signal. "If you like Chinese food, that place is really good." Then she wished she hadn't said anything, because the restaurant was actually a little pricey. "So's the Weaver Town Buffet in Weaver, though. They don't have real tablecloths, but you can get twice the food for half the price." She knew she was babbling. "This is where you turn."

She felt pretty silly stating the obvious, so she clamped her teeth together, determined to just be quiet.

The light changed.

He turned and the truck engine growled a little as they started up Hill Street, not so imaginatively named since the street was, in fact, on a hill.

She glanced over her shoulder, looking out the rear window. At least there was no sign of black exhaust spewing from the tailpipes. She sat forward again. "Got the exhaust fixed, I see. Where'd you take it?"

"Nowhere. Fixed it myself."

"Nice. Wish I could have done the same myself with my transmission. Wouldn't mind not owing money I don't have just *once* in a while. We're totally stalled right now on renovating the house until we can pool together more money." She clamped her fingers under her thigh, as a reminder to stop it from bouncing so nervously. "It's, uh, it's the house at the end of the block."

He pulled up to the curb in front of what had once been a grand lady. Now, it was simply a three-story money pit.

"That is an ambitious house," he said.

"Yep." She eyed it fondly. The snow was piled around it, adding a touch of frost that helped take one's eye away from the peeling paint and the other signs of aging. "Everyone thought we were crazy when we bought it. Particularly my dad. Said we would be throwing good money after bad for the foreseeable and unforeseeable future. I love it, though." She grinned. "Even the ghosts who steal our tools. Greer insists that I'm just too scatterbrained when it comes to keeping track of them, and I know it's not her or Maddie. So, unless it's our neighbor, Mrs. Gunderson, it's got to be—"

"Ghosts." He looked amused.

"Right. Want to come in and see it?" It was the first Monday of the month, so Greer would be at work until that evening, when Ali, Greer and Maddie planned to get together for dinner. "I've got *real* coffee."

His gaze slid over her. "Temptress." But he shook his head and she was more than a little alarmed by the lead balloon that sank in her stomach. "I'll have to meet the ghosts later."

"Sure." She hesitated before pushing open the squealing door. "I'll let you know what I find out about that phone number." She wondered just how involved he still was with his ex-wife. If, like with Jack, the relationship wasn't as finished as the term *divorced* implied.

"You can leave the message on my cell phone."

For some reason, she'd assumed he didn't have one.

"Okay." She pulled out her own phone. "What's the number?"

He recited it and she saved it in her phone, then stuck it back in her purse. "All right." She briskly climbed out of the truck. "I'll be in touch." She started to close the door.

"Ali."

He didn't say her name very loudly, but she still heard it above the screech of metal hinges. She looked at him through the wedge of open space. "Yeah?"

"Is it jumpy in a bad way? Or jumpy in a good way?"

She instantly felt like they were back in his upstairs hallway and her mouth went dry. "Good."

His eyes were steady on her face. "All right then."

She swallowed and moistened her lips. "All right then."

He smiled slightly. Then he reached across the bench seat and pulled the door out of her lax fingers, shutting it the last few inches.

She barely had the presence of mind to step back from the curb before he drove away.

When the sound of his engine faded, she was still standing there, her heart pounding beneath her coat.

"Good morning, Ali." Mrs. Gunderson, bundled in a wool coat that was probably just as ancient as she was, paused on the opposite side of the street while her leashed miniature black poodle, Mignon, did his business in the snow. "Everything all right?"

Ali dropped her hand. "Just fine, Mrs. Gunderson."

"Who was your friend?" Mignon had finished, and now jumped against his mistress's legs until she picked him up. "Oh, you fat little thing. I don't recall seeing that pickup before."

Rather than stand there yelling across the street, Ali crossed to the other side. "His name's Grant," she said when she reached the curb. "He's from Oregon. Moved out to the old Carmody spread."

"I remember the Carmodys." The elderly woman shook her head and the pink scarf tied around her neatly coiffed hair slipped down over her forehead. "That was a nasty business the way they lost their ranch to the bank."

"Mmm." Ali scratched Mignon's head and the dog's button-bright black eyes rolled.

"Can't really blame the economy for it," her neighbor went on. "Though that surely didn't help. But their luck was never good. Particularly after that unsavory business with their daughter."

That got Ali's attention. "Oh?"

"Of course, back in those days, babies born on the wrong side of the blanket still caused a bit of scandal." She dumped Mignon in Ali's hands while she adjusted her scarf and tied it again beneath her chin. "But is a little scandal worth all that trouble?" She clucked her tongue as she took back her little dog and set him on the ground, where he immediately started whining. "Now, Mignon. You have to walk! Dr. Taggart said you *had* to lose some weight!" In her typical way, she barely drew breath between thoughts. "The way they kicked their own daughter out of the house was just shameful, much more shameful than having a baby out of wedlock. Come along, Mignon." She tugged on the leash. "I'm determined that we'll walk to the bottom of the hill and back every day until he loses a couple pounds."

Ali wanted to pump Mrs. Gunderson for more information about the Carmodys, but she was sidetracked by concern for her neighbor. None of them knew exactly how old she was, except that she was somewhere north of eighty and south of a hundred. "It's a pretty steep hill, Mrs. Gunderson." She slid her purse strap diagonally across her body and slipped her arm through her neighbor's. "How about I walk with you?"

Mrs. Gunderson just laughed and disentangled her arm before turning her old-fashioned black snow boots downhill. "You're a sweet girl, Ali. But the day hasn't come yet when I can't walk my own hill. Go on, now. I know this is your day off."

Resigned, Ali watched the woman walk away. Mrs. Gunderson wasn't going to win any speed records, that was for sure, but she was making steady progress all the same.

After several minutes, Ali pulled out her cell phone and called the department, asking that a patrol car run by the bottom of the hill, just in case Mrs. Gunderson decided she wanted a ride back up it.

Then she crossed the street, sat down in the rocker on the front porch and kept watch over her neighbor from this end.

But that left her thoughts to roam.

And they roamed straight to Grant.

She had resources at the department that she could use to peek into Grant's personal life. At the very least, she could find out what happened with his biological family. It seemed to be fairly common these days for adopted children to voluntarily seek out their birth families once they were adults, whether it was to have their questions answered, get a sense of closure or forge a new relationship. Grant's motives didn't seem to fit any of those molds.

Maybe there were answers she could find on her own.

But when it came to him, she knew she couldn't do it. Go around his back like that.

She honestly didn't know whether that worried her or not.

Chapter Eight

"Here." Maddie had barely made it into the kitchen later that evening before she plunked Layla in Ali's lap and raced out of the room again, shedding coat and gloves as she went.

Ali looked over the baby's blonde head at Greer, who was also sitting at the table in the unfinished room.

Her sister returned her look with a shrug. "Got me," she murmured, and turned her attention back to the law book she was reading.

It was the first Monday of the month, which meant the three sisters were having dinner together. It was the one time that they all seemed to agree was sacred. Particularly since Maddie had moved in with Linc. Neither work nor husbands nor law books were supposed to get in the way of it. Unfortunately, that was all a fine idea in theory, but they hadn't managed a proper First Monday in months.

But that didn't stop them from trying.

After Ali had finished watching Mrs. Gunderson and Mignon return safely to their home, courtesy of two of Braden's finest, who'd just happened to be driving past the bus bench where a winded Mrs. Gunderson had been sitting, she'd left messages for both Greer and Maddie to remind them what day it was. Then she'd loaded up the slow cooker, remembering to turn it on this time. The one-pot concoction now actually smelled somewhat like what it was supposed to be—teriyaki chicken.

She worked Layla's arms out of her furry white coat and freed her from it, turning the tot to stand on her legs. The baby smiled gummily and Ali's heart just simply squeezed. "You're too sweet, you little chunk." She kissed her round cheek, then her sweet-smelling neck.

Layla chortled.

"Don't eat the baby," Greer drawled. "Give her to me."

Ali made a face. "Oh, I do not think so." She stood up, holding the baby on her hip. "Auntie Greer has always thought she can tell me what to do," she confided to the baby.

"For all the good it's done." Greer's voice followed Ali as she left the kitchen and headed into the living room.

She sat down with the baby on the dated shag rug that partially covered the parquet wood floor. What with all the trips Ali had made chasing "Daisy" Cooper's trail, combined with working nearly every minute when she was home, they'd made absolutely no progress on their restoration project.

The last thing they'd done was agree on a paint color for the kitchen.

Which still hadn't been painted. Not in Svelte Sage or any other hue.

Grant's walls were still unpainted, too.

She reached for the box of the baby's favored toys. She dragged it closer, pulling out the bright blue and red plastic bowls, and laughed softly when the baby immediately grabbed for them both.

"Whew." Maddie came into the living room and threw herself down on the couch that had once resided in their parents' basement. She propped her feet on the coffee table. She looked at the fireplace. "Fire feels good."

"Greer started it just a few minutes ago." Layla threw the red bowl and Ali grabbed it before it could roll too far. "Look at that arm." She wiggled the bowl and the baby snatched it again. She knew from experience that Layla could play this particular game endlessly.

"I'm pouring wine," Greer yelled from the other room.

"Yes," Ali yelled back.

"Pass," Maddie added, equally loudly. She returned Ali's look with an innocent shrug. "What?"

Ali lifted her shoulders. "Nothing." None of them drank a whole lot, but they generally managed to consume a bottle or two on First Monday. "What's the studly husband doing tonight?"

"Having dinner with his mother." Maddie folded her hands over her stomach and her head lolled back against the couch. "How's life with the Growler been?"

Ali shuddered.

Maddie smiled.

"You look tired."

"I am." But her sister sat up and pulled her feet from the coffee table when Greer came into the room carrying wineglasses and an uncorked bottle. She set everything on the coffee table, then pulled the water bottle from where it had been tucked under her arm and dropped it beside Maddie on the couch.

"Hope you showered today," Ali drawled.

Greer made a face back at her.

"Children, children." Maddie uncapped her water and held it out. "To First Monday. Finally."

"Amen to that." Greer and Ali picked up their wine-glasses and tapped them against Maddie's water bottle.

After a sip, Ali left the glass well out of Layla's reach and returned to the toss-the-bowl game.

"Keith Gowler was at the courthouse today," Greer said. "Looking as mopey as ever. What *did* you do to the poor guy?"

"Poor guy!" Ali made a face. "The man was talking about marriage and three-point-six kids on our third date. We had barely even kissed. And when we *did* kiss, I knew there wasn't going to be any chance of getting to the baby-making stage. Sloppy kisser."

"Eeeww," Greer said, and grimaced.

"Exactly."

Grant wouldn't be a sloppy kisser. The thought snuck in and Ali hurriedly threw up a mental block against it. "But I *did* have an excellent idea." She reached for the wineglass and pointed the rim of it in Greer's direction. "No smirks, Greer."

Her sister's eyes danced. She hid her smile behind her wineglass. Ali looked toward Maddie. "I just need to get Keith set up with someone new."

"Ahh—" Maddie hesitated, probably hunting for a tactful way of expressing the *"Oh, brother"* that Greer muttered.

It was always that way. Greer and Ali rubbed each

other wrong, and Maddie—the middle sister among the triplets—was the peacemaker.

"I'm serious. Think about it. Keith *so* wants to find a woman that he was willing to think I was the one!"

"Well, that's true," Greer allowed drily. "Maybe if you'd have kept dating him, he'd have come to realize his mistake."

"Oh, hah, Greer. Keith's not a bad guy. I went out with him more times than I should have, just because he's so infernally decent. We just need to think of a single woman who likes—"

"Sloppy kisses?" Maddie shook her head. "I don't know, Ali. Matchmaking? That kind of thing never works out."

"Please. Layla was the matchmaker for you and Linc." She wrapped the baby's hands in hers and clapped them together.

Maddie laughed softly. "Well, that did sort of work out," she agreed.

Greer caught Ali's eye. "Suppose she'll still have that besotted look on her face a year from now?"

"Oh, I expect I will," Maddie answered.

"You look like the cat who's gotten the cream," Ali accused.

"She's a newlywed," Greer said, smiling wryly. "They're probably doing it like rabbits."

"You're just jealous," Maddie returned. "Both of you. When's the last time *you* saw a nekkid man, eh?"

Greer laughed over her wine. "Ooh. Nekkid. Legal meaning? Without clothes and up to no good."

"And it is very, very good no-good," Maddie drawled.

Greer made a face. "Don't rub it in on your poor nunlike sisters. Last man I was with was—" she held her glass to the side as she considered "—criminy. Too long ago to admit even to you two. And Ali—"

"Saw a naked man today." She hadn't really planned to bring that up, but there was just something to be said for being able to make her two sisters sit up and take notice like that.

"No way!" Greer went from looking astonished to suspicious. "Not Keith. Dear God, please not—"

Maddie swatted her with her hand. She was looking at Ali. "You've got a new man? Finally! Why haven't you said something before now? I thought you were never going to let yourself get over Jack's—"

"I haven't *gotten* a man or anything else," Ali explained pointedly. "But I did see a naked man."

"Who?" Greer demanded.

She savored the name for a moment before saying it aloud. "Grant Cooper." Neither one had met Grant in person, but they certainly knew who he was.

Greer's eyebrows skyrocketed.

Maddie's jaw dropped.

Ali fanned her face. "And may I just say…*ooh la.*" Then she laughed and rolled onto her back. She held Layla up in the air above her and the baby gave a big, delicious belly laugh.

Greer scrambled around the coffee table and snatched Layla right out of Ali's hands.

"Hey!"

Her sister kissed the baby's fists and stared down at Ali. "Details, baby sister."

Greer had always lorded her thirty-minute age advantage over Ali.

"You're sleeping with the man who might be Layla's uncle?"

Ali looked at Maddie. "I'm not sleeping with him."

"But you would if you could," Greer said knowingly.

She wasn't going to deny what she wasn't sure she *could* deny.

"But clearly, you're getting…entangled here," Maddie persisted. "Do you think that's wise?"

"She's not worried about wisdom. She's worried about getting some action for her lady bits."

"And you're not," Ali retorted. She sat up and focused on Maddie. "It was a perfectly innocent accident, actually." She didn't elaborate, because if she did, she'd be admitting to the way she'd wristlocked the guy right out of his threadbare towel. Even though she'd flipped him inadvertently, that particular detail would not reflect very well on her. "And we were both embarrassed. Trust me. There is nothing going on between us except where Layla is concerned."

Maddie sighed faintly, but seemed to accept it.

Greer, however, was giving Ali the I-know-better eye.

Which just proved that Greer was better at spotting Ali's lies than Maddie.

"You *are* interested in him." Greer sat down on the coffee table, not seeming to care in the least when Layla butted her in the chin with her head and laughed as if she'd discovered a new game. "Not just sex-terested, either." She grinned. "Alicia likes a bo-oy," she mocked in a singsong voice.

"Grant's definitely no boy." Ali couldn't stop herself.

Greer's eyes danced. "I love it."

"Greer, don't encourage her!"

Greer turned on Maddie. "Why not? You said it yourself a few minutes ago, Maddie my dear. It's about time she got over Jack! Two-timing Ali *with* his ex-wife! He was a total weasel. If Grant *is* Layla's uncle, then

we've got a total lock on keeping her in the family!"
She bussed the big white heart positioned on the front
of Layla's stretchy red sleeper, then made a face and
quickly handed her back to Maddie. "Phew alert."

Ali saw the dark shadows under Maddie's eyes and
pushed to her feet. Not only was Maddie a newlywed
settling into the big old Swift Mansion with Linc, but
she was also still working full-time for family services
while taking care of the baby. Regardless of how the
situation had come about, she'd stepped into the role
of new mom without having nine months to get ready.
Was it any wonder she looked exhausted?

"I'll do it." Ali ignored both her sisters' surprised
expressions as she scooped up the baby and carried her
upstairs. They kept diapers and changing supplies as
well as a portable crib in Maddie's room for whenever
the baby was there.

She grabbed what she needed and set the baby in the
middle of the bed, wincing only a little as she changed
the messy diaper. "One of these days, I'll get used to
it," she promised the infant.

Layla didn't seem to care. She merely kicked her legs
merrily and chortled as Ali tried to wrangle her back
into a clean diaper and her red-footed onesie. The white
heart on the front reminded her of the robe that Grant
had pulled on that morning. "I really do hope he *is* your
uncle," she whispered as she carried the baby out of the
room and headed back down the stairs.

She raised her voice for her sisters' benefit. "If we
put our heads together, I'm *sure* we can think of a suitable match for Keith. It's just a matter of setting them
up without *seeming* to set them up." She reached the
bottom of the stairs.

Greer was once more sipping her wine. Maddie was sipping her water.

And Grant Cooper was sitting on the couch right between them.

Heat filled her face. She probably looked as bright a red as her co-worker Timmy had ever looked, and her sympathy for him went up about a hundred and ten percent.

Jumpy in a good way?

Heaven help her.

She swallowed the nerves suddenly pitching tents in her throat. "Grant. What are you doing here?"

"Got that address finally."

"Oh. Right." She shouldn't be disappointed that he'd come back because of that, particularly when it was one more possible clue to track down Layla's mother, but she was. She was wearing leggings and a Harry Potter sweatshirt and she felt unusually self-conscious as she carried Layla over to Maddie. "Great." She tugged at the hem of the sweatshirt. "I guess you've met my sisters." She gestured to each one in turn. "Greer. Maddie."

They were both smiling at him, though with entirely different tilts to their lips. Greer's expression was knowing, while Maddie's was wary.

Ali curled her hand over the baby's sweet head. "And this, of course, is Layla. Mom had her with her this weekend at the department. Grant happened to be there at the same time," she said to her sisters.

Maddie seemed to brace herself a little as she looked at Grant. Ali doubted that anyone but she or Greer would have noticed. "Would you like to hold her?"

He shook his head, looking as if she'd asked him to hold a land mine. Although, considering his CCT experience, he'd have probably been more comfortable with the land mine. "She doesn't know who I am," he said hurriedly.

Ali had to bite the inside of her lip to keep from smiling. Aside from Maddie, who'd always been good with babies and kids, they'd all had similar reactions to the baby.

At first.

"Come on into the kitchen," she invited. "I'll get that address from you."

He popped up from the couch like an overwound children's toy.

She sincerely wished that Maddie wouldn't look so worried, but she knew there wasn't a thing she could do about it. Maddie needed to take a leaf out of Greer's book. *She* was hiding her smile in her wineglass.

Ali led the way into the kitchen, seeing it through Grant's eyes. Unfinished cabinet frames with missing doors. Plywood countertop. Exposed plumbing. "I know. It's worse than your place." She pulled open the junk drawer and pawed through the mess for the notepad they used for their grocery and supply lists. She gave him a sideways look. "Only now I know you've got skills."

His lips twitched and she felt her cheeks warm.

"*Carpentry* skills."

He laughed softly and shivers danced down her spine. "I don't know about carpentry skills."

She finally latched onto the notepad and yanked it out. "Yeah, well, you say that, but you must be handy with your tools."

His eyes glinted even more. "Haven't had any complaints."

She blushed even harder. What was *wrong* with her? Just because it had been a while, she was no shy virgin.

"Just give me the address. You could have called me, you know. Saved yourself a trip."

"I could have."

She caught her tongue between her teeth, hoping she didn't look as ridiculously pleased as she felt. She might as well have been back in high school, having the senior quarterback ask *her*—not Maddie or Greer—to dance.

He pulled out his cell phone and showed her the text message.

Her schoolgirl euphoria ruptured.

The name of the sender was Chelsea.

She wrote down the Montana address, but left off the "XOXO" and the three hearts that followed it. Then she dropped the pencil back into the drawer and slammed it shut a little harder than necessary. "Chelsea is your ex-wife?" She remembered the first day they'd met. When he'd accused her of being sent by someone named Chelsea.

He stuck the phone back into his pocket. "Very ex," he said as if he knew what she was thinking.

She turned and leaned back against her hands on the drawer. She had to look up a long way to his face. And there seemed like very little space between them. Her heart was suddenly pounding, euphoria sneaking back in. "Are you sure?"

His eyes moved over her face. He slowly lifted his hand and lightly grazed his thumb over her lip. "Positive."

His head started to inch down to hers. "They have little flecks of yellow."

He paused. "What has little flecks of yellow?" he whispered back.

Her mouth felt dry and she swallowed. Moistened her

lips. "Your eyes." Maybe that's why they seemed aqua, rather than merely blue. Laser. Sharp. Blue.

He smiled slightly. "And yours are like chocolate. Dark. Melted. Chocolate. I've got a serious thing for dark chocolate."

She wondered if this was what it felt like to swoon. She heard his name sort of sigh from her lips, even though she hadn't consciously said a word. She swallowed again, leaning toward him—

"Yoo-hoo!" The back door flew open and Ali's mother blew in.

Ali jumped back. Grant merely lifted his head a little.

Feeling entirely cheated out of what she was certain would *not* be a sloppy kiss, she could only stare at her mother. Meredith hadn't really noticed Ali yet at all, since she was busy making sure that her mother-in-law, who was with her, made it safely up the back step. "What's going on?"

Meredith turned then, and seemed to notice Grant for the first time. More specifically, she seemed to notice how close he stood to Ali. Toe-to-toe. Her eyes turned even brighter. "Well, isn't this a nice surprise!" She left Vivian's side to approach them, extending a slender arm that was weighted down with a dozen delicate bracelets. "Grant. I'm Meredith—"

"I remember." He shook her hand. "It's nice to see you."

"What's nice to see is a fresh face around here." Vivian Archer Templeton shut the door with a hand firm enough to guarantee some attention. She was almost as petite as Ali's mom—who was even shorter than Ali and her sisters—but what Vivian lacked in height, she more than made up for in attitude.

Thanks to several wealthy dead husbands and Pennsylvania steel, she was richer than Midas. Ali and her siblings had never even met their grandmother, until a couple years ago when she showed up in Wyoming out of the clear blue sky intent on ending her estrangement with Ali's dad and uncle. Now, Vivian had a decent relationship with most everyone—except her sons. Even though she was opinionated, tended to veer between irreverent and arrogant and had a penchant for sticking her eccentric, aristocratic nose in everyone's business, Ali had become pretty darn fond of her.

Vivian picked her way across the floor as if the worn tiles would damage the soles of her expensive leather boots. She shrugged out of her fur coat and looked up at Grant. "You're a fine specimen, aren't you?" Her brown eyes were as bright as buttons and she patted her stylish silver hair. "Too young for me, but—"

"Vivian," Meredith chided.

Vivian's smile widened. She held out a beringed hand to Grant.

He looked at it for a second. "Do I kiss it or shake it?"

Vivian let out a sharp peal of laughter. She propped her hand on her slender hip. "Maybe you're not too young after all."

"Don't listen to her," Meredith said drily, grabbing Vivian's shoulders and forcibly steering her away from Grant. "She's more bark than bite, I promise."

Grant was smiling. "I think that might be a shame."

Vivian shrugged away from Meredith's hold. She clasped Ali's face between her hands. "If you don't know what to do with him, just tell your old granny, and I'll fill you in. I haven't buried four husbands without learning a thing or two."

Ali laughed wryly. Nobody called Vivian "granny." Hayley—who'd been the first one to show Vivian any welcome when she'd descended upon Wyoming—occasionally called her "Grandmother." To everyone else, she was Vivian. Pure, unadulterated Vivian. "I think I can manage," Ali assured her. And she would have been well on the way to proving it if not for the interruption.

She took Vivian's hands in hers and squeezed them very gently, because—for all of Vivian's larger-than-lifeness—she *was* a little frail. Not necessarily because she was on the high side of her eighties, but because she had an inoperable brain tumor. So far, it was causing only an occasional fainting spell. But they all knew it could cause something much worse. It could happen at any moment. Or it could happen not at all.

Vivian, of course, just took it in stride. She said that the thing had been squatting in her head for more than a few years now, and if the day came when it decided not to squat, well, then she'd finally be able to join "dear Arthur" at last. He'd been the fourth and final of her husbands and to hear her tell it, the only one she'd loved with all her heart.

"What brought you here?"

Vivian lived on the edge of Weaver, in a huge mansion she'd had built. It would have been more fitting for Pittsburgh, where she was from, than anywhere in the state of Wyoming, let alone Weaver.

Meredith unwound her winter scarf from her neck and unfastened her coat. "Vivian insisted."

And when Vivian insisted, woe to anyone who got in her way.

Ali focused on her grandmother again. "Because?"

"Because I'm on the Valentine's ball planning committee, and I wanted some fresh input from you young people."

"Valentine's Day is under two weeks away," Ali said warily. "Aren't the plans already in the works?"

"Yes, but I want to prove a point and there's no time to waste. Everyone on the committee is entirely stodgy." Vivian gestured at Meredith. "Including your bohemian mother, who is generally anything *but* stodgy." She eyed Ali. "Do *you* think the usual potluck in the high-school gymnasium is just fine?" She didn't wait for an answer. "Frankly, calling that a *ball* is a gross reach, if you ask me."

"We don't have a budget for anything else," Meredith reminded her.

"Bah." Vivian waved her hand and settled her fur on one of the kitchen chairs before perching on the edge of it. "I could take care of that with a snap of my fingers if there wasn't a certain dunderhead on the town council who has blocked every idea I bring to it."

"Dunderhead?" Grant asked.

"She means Squire Clay," Greer told him as she came into the kitchen with Layla to check out the fuss. She kissed Vivian's delicately lined cheek and then hugged Meredith, who promptly slipped the baby out of Greer's arms.

Ali couldn't help but notice the way Grant's gaze kept straying to the baby.

"You haven't been here long enough to know," Greer went on, "but Squire Clay—"

"Is intensely annoying."

Greer ignored Vivian. "Owns the largest ranch in the area—the Double C—and now he's also one of Weaver's council members."

"I'm sure he bought the election." Vivian tapped the table and her rings glinted under the bare lightbulb hanging from the ceiling fixture.

"You're still put out because he beat you for the seat last fall," Meredith replied calmly.

Grant looked at Ali. "Sounds like your grandmother has the hots for the guy."

Vivian's finely penciled eyebrows skyrocketed. "You're *obviously* new to the area, so I'll forgive you for that."

"Squire's first wife was our grandfather's sister," Greer disclosed.

"Vivian's first husband," Ali explained. "Vivian and Squire didn't get along then, and they don't get along now."

"What my granddaughter is being too polite to say is that I snubbed my husband's *half* sister ages and ages ago, because she was born on the wrong side of the blanket."

Ali jerked a little at the phrase. Not because it was news to her, but because Mrs. Gunderson had used it that very morning, too. Even if the women were from different locales, it just seemed proof that they were from the same era.

"But the only reason we don't get along *now* is because that old coot refuses to let an old woman apologize." Vivian pointed at Meredith. "He's no different than Carter and David."

"Don't blame me for that," Meredith said mildly. "Carter was your son before he was my husband." She jiggled Layla on her hip and smiled wryly at Grant. "Aren't you glad you brought it up?"

Grant's lips tilted in a smile. He looked at Ali. "Did I?"

"No, you did not."

"Tell me." Vivian looked Grant up and down. "Would *you* like celebrating Valentine's Day by sitting in some school building eating God knows what?"

"Can't say I've celebrated a lot of Valentine's

Days. And as long as the food doesn't come out of a government-issue pouch, I'm pretty good with it."

"That's not the answer I was looking for," Vivian said drily.

"Then you shouldn't have asked the question," Ali pointed out. She took Grant's arm and didn't have to work hard at all to steer him out of the crowded kitchen.

"Hey, I was gonna invite him for dinner," Greer called after them. Laughter was in her voice. "We're not eating out of pouches."

It was immediately apparent to Ali why Maddie hadn't also joined the fray in the kitchen. She was sitting on the couch, feet propped up on the coffee table. Sound asleep.

Ali rubbed her palm over the staircase's newel post. "You *are* welcome to stay for dinner," she told Grant softly. It seemed more than apparent that First Monday was once again derailed.

He shook his head, looking wry. "I mean this with the most respect, Officer Ali, but there's a little too much estrogen in there for comfort."

She grinned. "For me, too. But they are my family. Warts and all."

He glanced toward Maddie. "The three of you really *are* peas in a pod." Then he looked back at Ali and she shivered when his gaze seemed to drop momentarily to her mouth. "Rain check?"

She nodded. "Sure."

He smiled faintly as he grazed his thumb across her lower lip again. Then he plucked his coat from the back of a chair and quietly went out the front door.

Ali's knees had dissolved, and she sat down on the bottom step of the staircase.

"Alicia likes a bo-oy," Greer sang again from the kitchen doorway.

Ali propped her elbows on her knees and stared at the front door. "Yeah," she said on a sigh that was too dreamy for comfort. "Does she ever."

Chapter Nine

Looking into the Montana address Karen Cooper had given Grant's ex-wife to wire her money turned up nothing.

Ali sat at the desk she'd been assigned and stared blindly at the wall in front of her. Every single time they had a possible lead on Grant's sister, it ended up going nowhere.

Gowler dropped a file folder on her desk. "Get over to Braden Drugs. Manager reported a shoplifter. When you get back, type up these reports."

The folder was thick, meaning she'd be typing for some time—which was not her forte. But she wasn't going to complain since at least she got to deal with an actual complaint first. "Yessir." She grabbed her jacket and the keys to her unit before heading toward the door.

"Templeton!"

She paused.

"Take Timmy with you."

Great. She looked across the room at the other officer, who'd looked up from the book he was reading at the sound of his name. "Let's roll, Timmy."

His face turned red, but he grabbed his coat and they went out the back to where the department's vehicles were all parked. Ali drove, wishing there was something she could do to make Timmy relax around her.

"Timmy, you've got a sister, right? Still lives in town here? Single?"

He gave her a quick look. His Adam's apple bobbed. "Tracie. Yeah."

"Tracie got a boyfriend?"

He made a face. "Yeah. He's a jerk."

Keith Gowler wasn't a jerk. Just a sloppy kisser. Which might well be one of those beauty-in-the-eye-of-the-beholder things. "They serious?"

"I hope not," he muttered.

"She teaches over at the elementary school?"

"Yeah." His face was like a beet. "Why?"

"No reason." She smiled at him, wondering how on earth she could maneuver a "meet cute" between an elementary-school teacher and a defense lawyer. "Just making conversation." She turned into the parking lot of the small strip mall where the drugstore was located. The drugstore was at one end. Hardware store at the other. A dress shop and a bakery in between. Timmy called in their location and they went inside.

The girl at the counter jerked her head toward the back. "Manager's got him back in the office."

"Thanks." Ali led the way to the rear of the store. She knocked once on the closed door and then opened it.

The sight of the teenage boy sprawled in a chair made her cluck her tongue. "Trevor Oakes." She hadn't had an encounter with the kid since she'd rousted him out of Grant's vacant ranch house last year. "What's the deal?"

The store manager—a teenager only a few years older than Trevor—gestured at the array of products sitting on his desk. "He was shoveling all of this into his coat pockets. That's what the deal is."

Ali studied the items. Nothing there that he could cook with. Which was a relief. She didn't want to have to call in Trevor's poor mom to tell her that her son had graduated to making meth. "Nothing you can huff or puff here, Trev." She picked up a candy bar from among the other innocuous items. Visually, he didn't appear to be stoned, but that meant nothing. "Or do you just have the munchies?"

He made a face, crossing his arms. He clearly had no intention of answering.

"All right." She looked at Timmy. "Bag up the evidence, Officer. Let's take him in and process him."

To Timmy's credit, he didn't argue, even though they typically dealt with juvenile shoplifters at the scene. They rarely brought them in, even if charges were ultimately filed.

She gestured at Trevor. "Get up. Face the wall. Hands behind your back."

Finally, there was a hint of nervousness in his eyes. He did what she said and she cuffed him. "That your coat on the chair?"

He grunted an answer.

She gave him a look. "What's that?"

His jaw flexed. "Yes."

"Better." She tossed the coat over his shoulders. "You can come in and sign the complaint anytime this afternoon," she told the manager, who was watching with round eyes and slack jaw.

Then she walked Trevor, cuffed for all of Braden Drugs to see, out of the store. She put him in the back of the SUV behind the grill and as she waited for Timmy to catch up, she saw Grant walking out of the hardware store. He had a large bag propped on his shoulder.

Timmy still hadn't come out of the drugstore, but she drove across the parking lot, right in Grant's path.

Her heart wriggled around in her chest a little when he stopped and smiled at her.

She rolled down her window. She saw that he was carrying cement. "Looks like you're moving on from kitchen cabinetry."

"Yup. Spent the morning hunting down water lines. Now I get to repair the mess I made and put down tile again." He angled his head, looking at the occupant in her backseat. "Exciting day for Braden's finest?"

"Something like that." She couldn't seem to get the smile off her face. "No more cold showers?"

He stared into her eyes. His were slightly amused… and entirely mesmerizing. "Not without reason, anyway."

Every day since they'd had the snowstorm had been just a little warmer than the day before. And right then, it felt like the middle of a long hot summer to Ali.

She rolled down the passenger window, letting more winter air in to cool her cheeks. "I checked out the address you gave me." Better to stick to that, than let her imagination run amok. "Turned out to be a boarding-house owned by a woman named Honey Holmes." The name clearly meant nothing to Grant. "She rented a room to your sister for a couple weeks. But she cleared out after only one. The owner didn't have any idea where she was heading." She left out the part that Daisy— which was the name she'd rented the room under—had also left without paying the second week's rent. "Ms. Holmes did confirm that your sister was pregnant at the time. To use Honey's words, 'not quite ready to pop but getting there.'" She'd also called Daisy a tramp, but Ali figured she didn't need to share that detail.

"Maybe she had the baby in Montana."

"Possible. I've got a request in to check the birth records in Butte for the three months following her stay there. It's likely to be a lot, but maybe something will stand out."

Timmy jogged up to the truck then. He was carrying a paper bag that presumably held the confiscated stolen goods. He set it on the floor between his feet when he climbed into the vehicle.

"Talk later?" Grant suggested.

She nodded. It was silly that two words caused such giddiness to flow through her veins. "You could collect your rain check."

"Your kitchen or mine?"

She didn't have to even think about it. "Yours." She waited a beat. "It's in better shape than mine." They'd also be less likely to be interrupted by sisters or mothers or eccentric grandmothers.

His eyes glinted as if he knew exactly what she was thinking. "Come prepared. I have a big appetite."

She felt herself flush. Responding in kind was out of the question. Judging by the look he gave her, he knew it, too.

She waited until he'd crossed to his rusty pickup truck before putting the SUV in gear again.

"Who's that guy again?"

She glanced at Timmy. "Grant Cooper. He bought the Carmody ranch." It was nobody's business but Grant's that the Carmodys had also been his biological grand-parents.

"Oh, right." Timmy clicked his seat belt into place as she turned out of the parking lot and headed back to the department. "Steve said he'll come by and sign the complaint when his shift ends."

"Hey!" Trevor kicked the back of her seat. "I'm supposed to get a phone call or something, aren't I?"

"Sure, Trev. Soon as you're through processing." Which she intended to make as uncomfortable as possible. Maybe if she did the job well enough, Trevor would think twice before pulling his next stunt. "What do you think your mom's going to say when she has to come down and bail you out of jail?"

"You're not gonna put me in jail," he scoffed. "Stuff wasn't worth nothin'."

"Stuff worth nothin' can still get you up to six months, Trevor. Store manager caught you red-handed. We also got the surveillance tape, right, Timmy?"

"Right." Timmy made a face at her, which Trevor fortunately couldn't see. Because there was no surveillance tape. Not unless the drugstore had replaced their equipment since their last shoplifting episode, and she doubted it. The owner of the store was too cheap. Despite their recommendations, he maintained that the sight alone of a security camera was enough to deter would-be thieves. "Watched it myself." Timmy said it so convincingly that Ali was impressed. "Got him dead to rights."

She braked at the stop light and looked over the seat at Trevor. "Your mom's a pretty lady. She'll be really popular when she goes to visit you down at the prison in—"

"Prison!" Trevor's young face paled.

She faced forward again, leaving him to stew on that for a while.

When they got back to the department, she turned him over to Jerry. The older officer was a dad to two teenage boys about Trevor's age. He'd do a good job finishing what they'd started, and with any luck Trevor would see the value of returning to the straight and narrow.

Then she sat back down at her desk and flipped open Gowler's thick file of handwritten reports. But even the unappealing task of typing them up didn't bother her too much.

Not when she had Grant's big appetite awaiting her.

The sight of Ali on his doorstep that evening caused more pleasure than Grant expected.

If the winsome smile she was giving him was anything to go by, he figured the feeling was at least a little mutual. "I come bearing dinner." She held up a wide, flat pan with a blue-and-white-striped towel folded on top of it.

He started to take it from her but she looked down and nodded toward something. "Why don't you get that instead?" She didn't wait for an answer, but scooted past him into the house.

Another box sat on his porch.

More books.

Dammit, Chelsea.

He brought the box inside and shoved it in a closet. He'd lit a fire in the newly inspected fireplace and the box would have made good fuel. But it also would likely garner more curiosity from Ali than he wanted.

"When'd you paint in here?" She stood in the doorway to the kitchen, unfastening her puffy red coat. "Looks great."

"Last night." After he'd tired of staring at his ceiling while sleep eluded him. He took her coat from her and tossed it on top of the packing crates he still hadn't dealt with. "Needs another layer of paint, though. I can still see the shadow of graffiti showing through."

"If you say so. Personally, I can't see it, but—" She shrugged. Since he'd run into her that afternoon, she'd changed out of her uniform into jeans and another waffle-weave shirt—black, this time—and taken down her hair. The streaky locks waved around her neck. Her shoulders. Her breasts. "Did you get your cement work done?"

"I got it poured. It'll be a while before it's ready for me to tile. Meanwhile, I have a butt-load of painting still to do." He looked past her to see the blue-and-white-striped towel sitting on the counter. "What's in the pan?"

"Nothing fancy. Just a casserole. I stuck it in the oven to keep warm. Hope you like chicken, because if you don't, I'm not sure the pizza place will deliver this far outside of town. I do have these, though." She lifted a plastic bag full of cookies. "Almond-fudge drops. Best ever." She set it down on top of the towel.

"Cookies're always welcome." He held out his hand. "Hand 'em over."

"Didn't your mother tell you that dessert comes *after* dinner?"

He grinned. "Some situations call for different rules." He pulled out a cookie. They were small. It took three of them just to make up a proper bite. "Not bad," he said when he swallowed the delicious little bits. They had a dollop of frosting and little bits of almonds on top. "Who made 'em?"

"I beg your pardon?" She snatched the bag away from him like a punishment. "I did!"

Her indignation made him smile even more. Regardless of what brought her to his door, he knew he'd smiled more since he met her than he had in the last year. At least. "That stuff in the oven'll keep a while, then?"

"Should." Her eyes sparkled. "Why? You want to put a paint roller in my hand first?"

He slid his hand meaningfully around her waist and pulled her close, enjoying the way sparkle turned to melted chocolate. He took the cookie bag from her and tossed it onto the counter. "Maybe later."

Her hands flattened against the front of his sweatshirt. But she didn't push him away and the corners of her lips rose in a slight smile. "I don't sleep with strange men," she warned softly.

"Neither do I." He lowered his head toward hers. "You smell good. What is it?"

"Soap." Her voice dropped. Turned husky in a way that would have had all his nerve endings standing at attention if they weren't already. "You smell good, too." Her hands moved up his chest and linked behind his neck.

He brushed his lips over her temple, then skimmed down along her cheek. "Soap," he murmured against her ear. He kissed her shoulder and her heat radiated through the soft, textured shirt.

"Grant—"

He lifted his head and linked his hands behind her back. "Yes?"

She sighed a little, then suddenly melted into him.

"Hell with it." She pulled on his head, lifting her mouth toward his. "Kiss me, already."

"That was my intention. Good to know we're on the same page," he murmured and lightly grazed one corner of her lips with his. Little more than a whisper.

She made a sound and her fingers slid from his neck into his hair. "I don't know what page you're on, but I'm a little further into the book."

He laughed softly and teased the other corner of her mouth.

She tugged lightly at his hair, making another impatient sound. "Come on now," she complained. "Don't make me get rough."

He spread his fingers against her spine, feeling every little ridge. "Gonna flip me on my back again?"

Her eyes met his. "You on your back does have merit." Then she dragged his head back to hers, boldly fastening her mouth to his.

He hadn't intended on getting her into bed. Not exactly.

But at that moment, it was the only thing he could think of. He lifted her straight off the ground and she twined those deceptively long, lithe legs around his hips, lips still fastened to his.

He turned and bumped his way through the doorway. "Sorry," he mumbled against the smile he could feel on her mouth.

Her answer was to slide one hand down the back of his sweatshirt. Bare palm against his spine, fingertips pressing into his skin. "Not sloppy at all."

He could barely think for the fire licking at his veins. "What?"

She dragged his mouth to hers again. "Hurry."

The top of his head felt like it was ready to blow.

Instead of heading toward the stairs, he just turned and pressed her up against the wall, managing in the process to send the stack of paint cans and supplies careening.

She gasped, half-laughing, when he yanked up her thermal shirt and thrust his hands beneath, making direct contact with that silky smooth source of heat. She wasn't wearing a bra and he filled his hands with her slight curves. Her hips cradled his where he pinned her against the wall, rocking against him. Inviting more.

He tore his mouth away, breathing hard. "I wasn't prepared for this."

She tugged her shirt over her head and tossed it aside, then started yanking at his sweatshirt. "Definitely not a Boy Scout," she said breathlessly and pulled his hand back to her breast after he finished the job and pitched his sweatshirt in the general direction of hers. "Fortunately, I was. Am."

"A Boy Scout?"

"Prepared," she said throatily, and reached between them, fumbling with his belt. "I'm on the pill and I have a clean bill of health, so unless you—"

She was a whirlwind, decimating his few remaining brain cells that were still functioning. "I'm good," he responded.

She let out an exhilarated laugh. "Well, we'll see, won't we?" She finally got the belt undone. His fly. Freeing him. She wrapped her hand around him.

Need was roaring inside him but he latched his fingers around her wrists, catching them both and pulling them away. "Wait."

"I can't wait." She pressed her open mouth against his throat. Her hips worked against his and she wriggled her hands free. "I don't want to wait." As if to prove it, she reached between them again, somehow managing to unfasten her own jeans. Then she was guiding him to her, shuddering out a greedy sound that was hands-down the most erotic thing he'd ever heard.

Muttering a breathless oath, he caught her hips, sliding his hands beneath her thighs.

"Hurry," she whispered again. "Hurry, hurry."

How could he do anything else when she was gloving him so tightly? She was hot and wet and her need for speed was a good thing because he didn't have a hope in hell of lasting for long. "The couch."

She groaned, shook her head. "Too far—" She broke off and her fingers raked down his spine as she clung even tighter. He could feel the shudders in the very center of her working their way outward, wave upon wave upon wave. She cried out and he slammed his hand against the wall above her head. His only sane thought was not to crush her, while the rest of him raced headlong straight into the storm.

"Tsunami," he muttered when he could finally form words again.

They were sprawled on the couch, which he vaguely remembered stumbling to.

"Hmm?" She rubbed the top of her head against his chin. She was lying across his chest, her hands on his heart, her cheek on her hands.

"Tsu-Ali," he joked.

She lifted her head a few inches, giving him a look from drowsy eyes. "I think *tsu* means *sea* and *nami* means *wave*." She lowered her head again, sighing deeply, which just pressed all her pretty curves more firmly against him. "Or something like that. I saw it on the internet, and goodness knows everything on the internet is *always* accurate."

"Ali-nami."

She laughed softly. "Macho CCT not only knows how to laugh, but he also has a silly sense of humor."

He kissed the top of her head. He'd laughed more around Ali than he had in years. Rather than admit it, though, he slid his palm slowly down her bare back. "Not very macho with my jeans twisted around my ankles," he said.

"Don't hear me complaining." She stretched again, slipping her thigh between his.

He wasn't sure he'd felt this randy even when he'd been a teenager. "How'd we manage to get all your clothes off, but not mine?"

"Dunno." She rubbed her head against his chin again. "Does it matter?" She shimmied a little against him. "Oh. Right there. Scratch right there."

He obediently scraped his fingertips lightly against her spine.

She practically purred. "Perfect."

The wood in the fireplace popped and flung a spray of sparks against the black mesh of the screen. "This is pretty perfect."

She lifted her head again. "I meant the scratching—" She broke off, her eyes softening. "Oh." She lifted her hand and slowly rubbed her fingertip over his lower lip. "Yes." Then she hauled in another deep breath and let it out, causing all sorts of interesting sensations along the length of him.

She noticed and, once again, she looked up at him. Her eyebrows rose a little. A smile that was fifty-percent satisfied female and one-hundred-percent sexy flirted around her lips. "Already?"

He slowly dragged his finger along her spine, watching the way her eyes flickered in response. "Evidently, I'm properly inspired."

"I'll say." She slid the rest of the way over him, making a good imitation of a clinging blanket. "That casserole in the oven isn't gonna keep forever," she warned. "It'll dry out if we're not careful." She arched just right, and he slid home.

Her lips parted slightly and she exhaled, long and slow.

It occurred to him that he could watch that expression on her face for a life of Sundays and not tire of it. "Darlin', let it turn to dust. I can wait. I've eaten a lot worse. And there's always the cookies." Holding her in place, he jackknifed up until they were sitting.

She hissed a little between her teeth, holding on to the back of the couch while he managed to extricate himself from the jeans without extricating himself from her.

And then he flipped her over, onto her back. He slid his fingers through hers and lifted her arms over her head while he pressed even deeper and watched her eyes go wide, then flutter closed while she let out that shaky, husky sigh.

Even though it would be so easy to race back into the wind-tossed sea with her, he made himself go slow. He gently kissed her lips. Kissed the thick, dark lashes against her creamy cheeks. Lashes that lifted after he stopped.

She stared up at him. "This is going to get complicated," she whispered. "Isn't it." It wasn't a question.

He thought about the box of books.

About his sister.

Layla.

"Life's always complicated," he murmured.
And then he kissed her again.
This time, there was no rush.
Just a long, slow trip to the inevitable.

Chapter Ten

"Much as I appreciate the sentiment, this is not going to work." This time, Ali was the one wearing the red robe with the big white hearts. Though she'd enjoyed the sight of Grant wearing it the other day, it truly did fit *her* much better.

"What're you saying?"

She eyed Grant, who was pretty much folded in half in the bathtub. He'd filled it with enough hot water to fog up the cracked mirror above the sink, but not enough to reach above his knees, all bent the way they were. It was hard to pretend she wasn't melting inside. "I'm saying there ain't no way you and I are both fitting inside that tub. Not at the same time." She leaned over and pressed a fast kiss on his lips, then cupped some hot water and tossed it over his head before straightening.

He looked so disappointed that she almost laughed. With water dripping down his thick, dark hair into his face and that pouty expression pulling on his ridiculously perfect lower lip, she had an instant image of him as a little boy.

The longing that struck inside her came out of nowhere. And frankly, it scared the stuffing right out of her.

Being lovers would be complicated enough, considering Layla. The last thing she needed to be doing was imagining little Grants with aqua-colored eyes running around.

So she waved her hand at him. "Come on. I'm the one who has to get her butt into work this morning."

"Speaking of butts." His hand snuck up beneath the terry-cloth robe and cupped her rear. "Have I told you just how much I appreciate yours?"

She sidled away from him, slapping at his hand, even though delight was coating the knot of want suddenly throbbing inside her. "I believe you made that apparent around three this morning." The chicken casserole hadn't been quite dust when they'd finally gotten to it the night before. But it had been more of a shovel-it-in-for-fuel than fine-dining experience. Then he'd wolfed down her cookies and tugged her up the stairs and into his bedroom.

When he pulled her down onto his bed, she'd discovered that the kisses he bestowed on every other part of her body besides her mouth weren't sloppy, either. She'd finally fallen exhaustedly asleep only to be awakened by the insistent nudge of his erection against her backside.

They'd had enough sex in the last twelve hours to fill her five-year drought, and then some.

She could hardly walk.

And she needed to get to work.

"I *need* the bath," she told him sternly. A shower would have been faster, but they couldn't use the one upstairs because the cement on the bathroom floor was still curing.

"Fine." Still endearingly pouty, he stood and water sluiced lovingly down his body, the level inside the bathtub dropping several inches.

She reminded herself that her body ached in places that it hadn't ached in ages. A delicious ache.

"Did you have to do a lot of swimming to qualify for combat control?"

He grabbed a thin, faded blue towel from the rack. "Enough," he said warily. "Combat diving. Parachuting. We did a lot of stuff. Why?"

"I read an article the other day about the men's Olympic swimmers. You've got the same kind of body. Perfect for swimming." Long arms. Roping muscles. Wide, flaring shoulders and a narrow waist, and those ripped abs.

She swallowed before she started drooling and shucked the robe. Carefully keeping a safe foot between them, she stepped over the side of the tub and sat down gingerly.

She didn't know whether to gasp or groan when the hot water hit her tender regions.

She glanced up at Grant. He was watching her with an expression she couldn't decipher. "What?"

He kneeled on the plain towel that Ali had spread on the floor in place of a bath mat. "You're sore."

She blamed the sudden heat in her cheeks on the temperature of the water.

"Hand me the washcloth," he said.

She warily handed him the cloth, which matched the towel he'd wrapped around his hips both in faded color and thinness. When he thrust it down into the water beside her hip, she jumped a little. "What—"

"Don't be so suspicious. Relax." He pulled the cloth back out and soaped it up, then slowly ran it over her shoulders and down her back.

Her resistance dissolved as her bones melted. She hugged her knees to her chest and rested her forehead on them while he repeated the process. "Nobody's ever washed my back." She smiled faintly. "Except my mother."

"I'm not your mother."

She turned her cheek until she could see him. "I'm well aware."

His aqua eyes darkened. "Lean back."

How—*how* could she be so easily aroused by him? When every muscle inside her had already been wrung with so much pleasure that she could have wept from it?

She stretched out her legs. Unlike Grant, she fit in the tub comfortably. She pressed her toes against the foot of the tub and lay back. The white enamel was chilly behind her neck and despite the water lapping at them, her nipples tightened.

Or maybe that was from the way Grant's gaze ran over her in the moment before he glided the soapy cloth over her shoulders and down the valley between her breasts. Then back up and over them, lightly dragging the vaguely scratchy terry cloth, making her skin feel even more deliciously sensitized.

Her mouth went dry as he tugged the cloth back into the water, then along her hip. Her thigh. Knee. He soaped her feet. Her toes. Smiled slightly when she curled her toes against the tickle of the rough cloth.

"You're frighteningly good at this," she murmured

when he'd reached across her to bestow the same attention on the left side of her body.

He sat back a little and touched the cloth to the base of her throat. The water had become cloudy from soap. It was more lukewarm than hot. "Is that a problem?"

She pressed her tongue against the inside of her teeth for a moment. "I don't know. Is it from practice?"

"Using soap and water? Been doing it all my life."

His hand had guided the cloth downward again. She caught his wrist before he reached her belly. "You know that's not what I mean."

"Have I ever washed a woman's back?" His eyes met hers. "Yes."

She couldn't blame him for answering the question that *she* had asked.

"Have I ever washed a woman's front? Yes."

She swallowed.

"I'm thirty-seven, Ali. I was married. And when I wasn't, there were others." His intense gaze was disturbingly steady. "Not going to pretend I was a saint and not going to brag that I wasn't. I'm not your first, either." He released the cloth and it sank in the water. He turned his hand and pressed his wet palm against hers. "But there hasn't been anyone in a long while. I haven't wanted anyone. Until now. Until you."

She shivered. And it wasn't because of the cooling water. It was because of him. His words. "Grant—" She broke off, not sure what exactly she wanted to say. She wasn't a verbal expert like Greer. Nor a relationship expert like Maddie. She just knew that there were things about Grant that drew her in. Physically. Emotionally.

And he was still waiting for her to finish.

She exhaled shakily and drew his hand into the

water. Toward her. Physical was easier than emotional. Always had been. "I'm going to be late for work."

He didn't smile. "Then we'd better make it worth it, right?"

And they did.

"Templeton!"

Gowler was yelling her name the very second she showed her nose at work.

She rolled her eyes at Timmy and hurried to the door of the sergeant's office. "Yessir?"

He was holding a file folder in the air. "What the hell're you doing messing with Draper's investigation about that abandoned baby your sister's fostering?"

She hesitated. "I, uh—"

"You're lucky I'm feeling magnanimous today." He tossed the file across his desk at her. "Next time you're late reporting, don't bother showing up at all."

She quickly retrieved the file folder. "I won't, sir."

He grunted. "Close the door on your way out."

She scurried out and closed the door.

Then she quickly flipped open the file folder.

Inside were her notes about births in Montana within the estimated time frame of Layla's birthday and she realized she must have gotten it mixed in with the reports she'd typed up for Gowler.

It seemed a lot longer ago than just the previous afternoon.

"What's wrong with you?" Timmy asked when she headed back to her desk.

She stopped short. "What do you mean?"

"You're walking all stiff-like. You hurt yourself working out again?"

Her cheeks went hot. "Um, yeah. Working out."

She slipped into her chair and jabbed her computer keyboard, bringing the blank screen to life. She went through her emails, which were all fairly routine. Then she checked the missing persons on Grant's sister. It had only been a week since she'd broadened the search to include Daisy's real name. She didn't really expect any results, and in that regard, she wasn't disappointed.

Her cell phone pinged, and she glanced at it, making a face when she read the brief note from Greer.

She swiveled around to look at Timmy. "Prosecutor's filed against Trevor Oakes."

"Yeah." Her coworker didn't look up from the book he was reading. "So?"

She threw an eraser at him and it bounced off his head.

"What?" He leaned over and grabbed the pink eraser and tossed it back at her.

She caught it. "Did you know about it?"

"Yeah. When Jerry was with him, Trevor hauled off and decked him."

All she did was stare at Timmy in shock. "That's what he's charged with? Assaulting a peace officer? Not petty theft?"

"Yep." Jerry walked into the squad room. He'd obviously overheard. "I tried to talk Gowler out of it, but half a dozen people saw it."

She sighed. He was already sporting a shiner. "I should have taken him home to his mother instead of bringing him here."

"It's not your fault, Ali." Jerry shrugged. "Kid just hasn't hit bottom yet. But he will."

"Hopefully sooner rather than later," she muttered. There were degrees of *bottom*, and for everyone's sake, she hoped Trevor's wouldn't be much deeper. He was still a minor, but an assault charge wasn't one they could just sweep under the rug.

"My sister didn't say when he was supposed to appear." Time was rarely slow in juvenile court cases. At least not in Braden, which was her only field of experience.

"Tomorrow morning at nine," Jerry said. He sat down at his desk, two over from Ali's, and tossed her a pink notepad. "Got a call yesterday after you left from some lady in Montana. Number's there."

Excitement warred with her concern over Trevor as she looked at the handwritten phone message. Jerry was old-school. He never texted and he used email only as a very last resort. He even refused to carry his cell phone with him, because he was adamant that they caused brain cancer. Instead, the thing sat—usually with a dead battery—on his desk. "Thanks." She swiveled around to face her own desk again and quickly picked up the phone, returning Honey Holmes's call.

"Mrs. Holmes!" Ali sat up straighter when the woman answered on the third ring. "This is Ali Templeton from the Braden Police Department in Wyoming. You phoned me yesterday?"

Honey sounded breathless. "Sorry, Detective. I've been changing sheets."

Ali didn't bother correcting the title. "What, uh, what can I do for you?"

"Come here and change the sheets for me?" Honey laughed ruefully. "You said I should call if I remembered anything else about that poor sad Daisy."

"Poor and sad" was an upgrade from "tramp." "Yes, I did." Ali automatically grabbed a sharp pencil from the cup of them she kept on her desk. "What do you have for me?"

"Well, one morning, she came down to breakfast. I serve breakfast every morning, you see. Nothing fancy, mind you. My people here are mostly hard workers who appreciate good, wholesome fare. You know. Oatmeal. And scrambled eggs. Good thick slices of toast. I make two loaves of country bread every day and—"

"That sounds really delicious, ma'am." Ali tapped the eraser end of her yellow pencil against her desk. "If I'm ever in Montana, I'll have to look you up. But about Dai—"

"Oh, my, yes. Well, as I said, she came down to breakfast late one morning and I was already starting to clean up."

Ali tapped her pencil a few more times, reining in her impatience.

"She must've been in a mood to talk," Honey went on, "because she started helping me clear the serving dishes. She mentioned that she used to waitress some-place in Wyoming. *Magic Mike*. Oh—" the woman tittered "—that's that racy movie about those dancing men. My daughter took me to it some time ago when it was playing in the movie house, and oh, my stars and body. What a show that is! Did you happen to see it?"

"Mrs. Holmes, please. Was the place she mentioned called Magic Jax?"

"Well, yes. Yes, I believe it was!"

Ali's shoulders sank. No new information at all. Which certainly wasn't Honey Holmes's fault. "Daisy was a cocktail waitress at Magic Jax over a year ago. It's a business here in Braden."

"Oh. You already knew that."

"That's okay. Remember, I said anything that you re-call would be important to me. And maybe you'll think of something else she happened to mention when she was staying there. Maybe about the baby. Or even the baby's father."

"Well, she just said that Grant would really hate her if he ever found out what she'd done."

Ali stiffened. "Grant?"

"I assumed he was her baby daddy. Isn't that the term they use nowadays? Young people having babies out of wedlock left and right. Not that it's anything new..." Ali closed her eyes, letting the woman rattle on, figuring that sooner or later, Honey would peter out.

And when she finally did, Ali's ear felt hot from the plastic receiver pressed against it for so long. "I really do appreciate your time, ma'am," she assured her. "Don't hesitate to call again."

"Well, I sure won't," Honey answered. "If you ever find that rapscallion Grant person, you tell him he needs to pay the week's rent that she still owes. You take care now, Detective."

Ali pinched the bridge of her nose. "You, too, Mrs. Holmes." Grateful that was over, she dropped the receiver onto the cradle and proceeded to drop her head onto her desk.

"What the devil's wrong with you?" Gowler stopped next to her desk, and she lifted her head in time to see him dump another pile of handwritten reports into her in-basket.

She sighed faintly and reached for the top one.

"Traffic first," he barked.

Her fingers curled.

In a contest between the dreaded typewriter and reading parking meters, she wasn't sure which was worse.

She waited until he returned to his office and slammed the door behind him.

Maybe Sgt. Gowler needed a woman in his life even more than his son did.

She swiveled around to look at Timmy again. As usual, he was still nose-deep into his book. "Timmy, honest to God, you read more than anyone I know." Except maybe Grant. He had boxes of books getting delivered right to his front door. Although she hadn't seen any evidence that he was actually reading in between installing kitchen cabinets, painting walls and loving her into a near coma.

Timmy's face was its usual shade of scarlet. But he held up the book so she could see the dark red cover. "Cal Reid," he said. "He's a great character. Right up there with Marlowe and Bosch and Rapp and—"

She lifted her hand. "The last book I read was a do-it-yourself on drywalling. I don't even know *who* you're talking about." She got up, knowing that she was moving stiffly but not able to do a darn thing about it. Lifting weights and doing chin-ups in her basement was one thing.

Nonstop hotter-than-Hades sex with Grant was on a different scale altogether.

She grabbed her coat and gloves, made sure her radio had fresh batteries and headed out to do traffic.

She supposed it could be worse.

It could be snowing.

She was still consoling herself with that fact two hours later as she trudged along the slushy streets, willfully ignoring most of the expired meters. When she spotted an ostentatious car parked crookedly at the curb in front of Sally's Treasures, though, she groaned. One of the wheels had jumped the curb and the corner bumper was kissing the meter post.

"Oh, Vivian," she muttered. Because, unless someone *else* in the area had taken to driving around a Rolls-Royce Phantom—which she highly doubted—the terrible parking job was owed to none other than her indomitable grandmother.

She checked out the meter post and decided it had survived the impact better than the bumper, which wasn't quite crumpled, but definitely bore a new scratch, and then headed toward the antique shop.

To this day, Ali wasn't sure how Sally stayed in business. As far as she'd ever been able to tell, the antiques that were crowded nose-to-toe inside the overly warm shop never seemed to change. But year-in and year-out, the shop remained, with Sally Enders sitting at the ancient cash register, usually hunched over while she carefully cleaned some ugly piece of jewelry she'd triumphantly found at an estate sale.

"Hi, Sally," she greeted when she went inside, quickly unfastening her coat. "My grandmother here?"

Sally barely looked up. She had a loupe clipped to her eyeglasses. "In the back."

"Thanks." She went straight to the rear of the store and pushed through the door that sported a Keep Out sign square in the middle of it.

And there was Vivian, poking her way around a jumble of chairs that were only fit for a bonfire. "Looking for more furniture for the palace?"

Vivian jumped a little. She pressed her lined hand against the front of her pink Chanel suit. "Lord, Ali. If this thing squatting in my head doesn't kill me, a heart attack will."

"Sorry." Ali kissed her cheek. "What *are* you doing?"

Evidently mollified, her grandmother quickly went back to her poking. "I need chairs," she said. "Lots and lots of chairs."

"For—"

"The Valentine's ball."

"The gym has chairs. Well," she amended, "benches, I guess."

Vivian gave a derisive snort and kept poking.

"It didn't look like you put any change in the parking meter outside."

"Parking shmarking."

Ali had to bite her lip. "You also came pretty *close* to the meter when you parked." There'd been a time shortly after Vivian moved to Wyoming when she'd paid a teenager to drive for her. Not a single member of her family didn't still wish that someone else was behind the wheel of the Rolls whenever Vivian wanted to go for a spin.

Her grandmother shrugged. "It's still standing, isn't it?" She'd managed to free one of the chairs from the tangle. "What do you think?"

At a loss, Ali looked at the chair. "I think whatever rear end sits on it is going to be touching the ground."

Vivian laughed. "You need to look beyond the obvious, darling."

"Vivian, you're talking over my head. The chair has two arms, four legs and part of a back. No spot to sit in. So to me, it's not much of a chair."

"It will be." Looking eminently satisfied, she gestured at the rest of the jumble. "When I'm finished, they all will be. And it will be simply grand."

"What will be grand?"

"The Valentine's ball, of course. Do try and keep up, dear." Vivian picked up her handbag from where she'd left it on a dusty bureau and tucked it in the crook of her elbow. She led the way back out to the shop, giving Ali a look. "Are you saddle sore or something?"

Ali nearly choked. "What?"

"You're walking like—oh, never mind. Sally—" Vivian raised her voice "—I want them all. Tell your son they need to be upholstered in that red velvet I gave you a sample of, and I'll want them delivered to my estate by next Saturday. How many did you say there were?"

Sally set aside her loupe and the ugly necklace she was working on. "Thirty-two."

"I'd hoped for more, but it'll have to do for now." Vivian smiled. "You know where to send the bill."

"Absolutely." Sally handed Vivian her fur coat, which had been hanging on a standing coatrack carved to look like elephant tusks. "Always a pleasure, Mrs. Templeton."

Ali hurried out the door after her grandmother. "Vivian, I'd dearly love to keep up with you. Did you get the planning committee to agree to this?"

"Please." She waved her hand dismissively.

Ali took that as a *no*. Knowing her grandmother, that was enough cause for concern. Vivian could spend money like nobody's business. Of course, that habit was mitigated somewhat by the fact that she was richer than sin. If Vivian wanted to throw her money away, it was hers to throw. "So...*you* are having a ball instead."

"Well, not a formal ball in the traditional sense." Her grandmother clasped her hands together and leaned against the side of her car. Parked among pickup trucks and SUVs, it looked particularly outrageous.

"I'm not exactly sure what a formal ball is in the traditional sense," Ali said drily, "but go on."

Vivian gave her a look. "Don't play dumb. You're merely trembling in those awful man-boots you wear, afraid that I'll require you to wear a ball gown."

Ali made a point of glancing down at her so-called

man-boots. They were entirely department-issue. But
she still took a little issue. At Christmastime, her grandmother had thrown what was becoming her usual fancy-
dress party. Ali had had to borrow a dress from her
mother, but she'd done it and shown up more or less
appropriately attired. "Just because I'm a cop doesn't
mean I don't like to wear pretty things," she said de-
fensively. "I just can't afford—"

"Bah. You could afford plenty if you'd just let me get
that hovel you live in fixed up for you."

"I'm not taking money from you, Vivian." It was an
old argument—Vivian wanting to give Ali and her sisters money to fix the place up right. And by that, Vivian meant right now.

"Instead, you insist on pouring what meager money
you *do* have right down leaking pipes."

She let the "meager" part slide, since it was more
than a little accurate. "In that, you and Dad agree."

"Well, that would be the *only* thing your father would
agree with me about. And David is nearly as bad."

Ali hurriedly changed the subject. Carter and David's
feud with their mother had been going on longer than
she'd been alive. While it wasn't entirely open warfare
between them, the way it had been in the beginning,
the rest of the family had pretty much accepted that it
wouldn't end anytime soon. "Back to the untraditional
nonformal ball."

Vivian's expression immediately brightened. "Oh,
yes. A ball on ice."

"Pardon?"

"Ice skating." She clasped her fur collar closer beneath her chin and her eyes danced. "Arthur took me
ice skating the first time he proposed to me. Oh, it was
magical."

Ali couldn't help but smile at the image that brought to mind. When her grandmother married Arthur Finley, she'd been in her seventies. Ali figured most people would be worried about falling and breaking a hip or something. But not Vivian.

"We'll have an ice rink. And a warming tent, of course, with every refreshment that Montrose can think of. He's in his element, I can tell you that."

Montrose was her grandmother's chef, brought with her from Pennsylvania. He was bald as a cue ball and as snooty as a dowager. Nevertheless, the things that came out of his kitchen were a taste bud's treasure.

"That's a lot to get underway in very little time, Vivian. Are you sure you're not taking on too much?"

"Delia's helping. She doesn't have the natural abilities that Penny had, of course, but she's coming along quite nicely, actually."

Delia was one of Ali's cousins. She'd never particularly been known for her consistency in life. But she'd been acting as their grandmother's personal assistant since before Christmas, ever since Penny, Vivian's previous assistant, had married Delia's big brother, Quinn. "Is Penny returning to work for you once she and Quinn are back from Texas?"

"They're already back. Good Lord, child. Don't you keep up with your own cousin and his wife?"

Ali wasn't going to get sidetracked. "Back to the chairs, Vivian. What are the chairs for?"

"Just because it's a Valentine's ball on ice doesn't mean guests won't need a place to sit." She plucked a pair of gloves from inside her handbag and started pulling them on. "It'll be a lovely sight. Women in old-fashioned dresses. Men in their ties and tails. It'll look like a Victorian postcard."

"In an area where dressing up basically means kicking the cow pies off your boots before going inside." Ali knew she sounded doubtful and couldn't help it. "That kind of fancy dress might be hard for some people to come by, you know. Particularly on such short notice."

"I know. Which is why I'm making sure that *some*—" she gave Ali a pointed look "—*are* accurately attired. I've already arranged for costumes to be sent out from Pennsylvania. My former dressmaker is handling it. The rest of my guests will simply make do. I'm certainly not going to turn them away from the event just because they aren't dressed right. The old me might have wanted to, but not anymore. All I'm asking for is that everyone who comes consider making a small donation to the Fielding Memorial Library Fund."

Ali felt a pain in her forehead. "I didn't know there was such a fund."

"There is now," Vivian assured her blithely. "Arthur was a strong believer in the public library system, and Weaver's is entirely inadequate. I mean to see that changed, starting with building a new library. And I could pay for it myself, but Hayley keeps reminding me that it's important for people to feel invested in their community. So." She clapped her gloved hands together. "I'm making this the start."

"What about the potluck that's already in the works?"

"It's the following day. It'll be fine. Delia has begun posting signs around town and she's already getting interest."

Vivian had all her bases covered. "I haven't been on ice skates in years, Vivian," Ali warned. As a girl, she'd played hockey with the boys and always figured she'd had more fun than the girls prancing around in their white figure skates. "And never while wearing some froufrou skating dress, much less some old-fashioned outfit straight out of a Dickens novel."

"Skating'll come back to you."

"I'm glad *you* think so," she said drily. "Where is this postcard rink supposed to be? Weaver has a skating rink already."

"Yes, and they play *hockey* on it. Dreadful sport." Oblivious to Ali's reaction, she plowed on. "The rink will be created behind my house. I already have it worked out with my landscape architect. It'll be like nothing Weaver has ever seen."

Ali nodded. "That's for sure."

"And you'll bring your handsome Grant. He'll be a fine escort, I'm certain."

Ali's lips parted. "I don't know if that's something he'll be particularly interested in, Vivian."

Vivian gave her a sidelong look. "I'm sure you'll find a way to convince him." She had her keys out now and they jangled as she waved gaily and hurried around to the driver's side of the car.

"Vivian, *please* be careful driving."

"I'm always careful, darling." She got inside and a moment later, revved the engine. The window on the passenger side rolled down.

Ali stepped closer, looking inside the car. "What?"

"Try Epsom salts in the bath," Vivian advised, looking crafty. Then she rolled up the window, bumped off the curb and shot down the street.

Chapter Eleven

"How far did you get reading that *Plumbing for Dummies* book?"

Grant looked up from the liver and onions he'd ordered for lunch and felt something lift inside him. It was barely more than twenty-four hours since he and Ali had sloshed bathwater all over his bathroom floor. "If it isn't Officer Ali. Young Timmy told me you were over at the courthouse when I stopped in." He lifted his fork. "I'd offer you some, but I know how you feel about this stuff."

She grinned and slid into the booth opposite him. Without asking, she did, however, reach for his cup of coffee and take a sip, squinting a little over the steam rising from it. "As a matter of fact, I was at the courthouse."

"You look pretty happy about it."

"Only because of the ironies of fate."

He raised his eyebrows.

She laughed softly and leaned toward him across the table. "I told you about Keith."

"Yeah. You also told me your movie-of-the-week plot."

"Which you scoffed at," she reminded him. "And yet…" She sat back, spreading her slender palms wide. Her dark eyes sparkled.

"You actually set him up with someone."

"That's the beauty of it." She was practically wriggling in her seat with excitement. "I didn't have to!"

"Hey there, Ali. Bring you some lunch?"

Ali looked up at Josephine. "Um, sure. The French dip. But only if it's fast. I've got to get back to the department before Gowler notices I'm not still at court."

"Coming right up," Josephine assured her before hustling back to the kitchen.

"You didn't have to set him up."

"Nope. Keith's pulling public-defender duty this week and got assigned a juvenile we hauled in a couple days ago. He took one look at the boy's mama and—" she spread her fingers "—*poof.* Love was in the air."

"Just like that."

"Hey. It happens."

She didn't need to tell him. Once Cal and Talia had scooped him out of the bowels of perpetual unwantedness, Grant had listened dozens of times to their love-at-first-sight story.

Even then, he'd never been a particular believer. He'd always figured that lust at first sight was probably closer to the truth of it.

And *that* he could seriously believe in.

"Maybe," he said. "So long as it helps get Gowler off your back, why not?"

"Oh, I promise you. I recognized the signs on Keith's face." She fluttered her lashes. "By the time Judge Stokes cracked his gavel on the case, Keith was giving Lydia Oakes the most besotted looks you've ever seen."

"Besotted?"

She nodded. "Besotted. Sarge is *definitely* going to be hearing about his boy's latest love interest." Her knee brushed against Grant's beneath the table. "So about that plumbing."

He eyed her, genuinely amused. "That's some pretty seductive talk there, Officer."

She leaned across the table again. "It's not a euphemism!"

He laughed, drawing glances from the other diners.

She grinned and sat back again. Her eyes clung to his and he wondered if the onlookers would describe *them* as besotted. Then he wondered if he even cared. "Isn't Stokes the judge in charge of Layla's case?"

She nodded. "And speaking of Layla, I learned there were roughly forty female births in the general area during the three months after your sister was at the boardinghouse in Butte. If I want statistics more recent than that, it's going to take a trip to the recorder's office there."

"And?"

"None of the mothers' names was Karen Cooper or Daisy Miranda. But if she used one alias, she could have used another. It's a matter of tracking all the families down and, well…" She made a face. "You know how it is. Not enough hours in the day."

"Situation calls for a private investigator."

"Yeah, and I'd need a mint to print some money to pay one, too."

The truth sat coiled inside him. If he was any sort

of decent brother at all, he would have contacted John
Fletcher to track down his sister when he'd first learned
about Layla. John had done plenty of other work for
him. "Your brother-in-law's got money. And a vested
interest."

"Yeah, but because Linc *does* have a vested interest, they need to avoid the appearance of trying to ma-
nipulate the situation. It was touchy enough for him to
foot the bill for the trips I've already made. Same thing
with my grandmother. She'd do anything she could to
help Maddie and Linc. She'd even consider bribing a
judge. She didn't, thank God." She rolled her eyes ex-
pressively. "But that's why the detectives are handling
the investigation."

"Who haven't done squat. You're the one who tracked
Karen to me."

"And that's as *far* as I've gotten, which hasn't helped
much. We still don't know for sure that Karen is Layla's
mother, and we have absolutely *no* idea who the father
might actually be. The lady in Butte remembered your
sister mentioning your name, and she assumed *you* were
the dad."

He grimaced. "I'm from a twisted family, but not
that twisted."

Ali eyes rested on his face and he wished he hadn't
said that. Fortunately, she seemed to sense his dis-
comfort and after a second, she went right on. "She
also relayed that Daisy said you would really hate her
if you found out what she'd done. Do you suppose she
meant getting pregnant?"

"Who knows?"

"There are just so many blanks that need filling in."

"Anyway." She took another sip of his coffee. Setting
the cup back next to his hand, her fingertips brushed

against his. "The investigation has gone beyond what's normal in this situation. It's a miracle that Stokes hasn't already placed Layla for adoption. Truthfully, I think he's got a soft spot for Maddie."

"But not soft enough to put your sister's name at the top of the adoption waiting list."

"Not if he wants to keep getting reelected. It's one thing to push the envelope and another thing to toss it out entirely."

"Here you go." Josephine had returned in record time. She set a loaded plate and a tall glass of water in front of Ali. Then she was off again.

Ali immediately picked up the roast-beef sandwich and dunked it deeply into the cup of juice nestled in a mountain of crispy French fries. "Great French dips here," she murmured, and shoved the dripping sandwich into her mouth, taking a huge bite. She swallowed quickly, barely seeming to chew first. "So about the kitchen faucet. Totally flipped its lid this morning. Water was spewing everywhere, which makes me glad we *haven't* gotten the cupboards finished, or we'd have that mess to deal with all over again. Maddie knows how to replace the faucet and the pipes leading to it, but she's so busy with Layla and Linc and her job, I don't want to bug her."

"Do all social workers know how to plumb a sink?"

"I think if they work around these parts they do," Ali said. "I can manage it myself, I think, but I don't have the tools."

"Ah. The crux of the matter." He was glad to change subjects to something else besides Karen having her baby alone in Montana. If he'd been there for her, none of this would be happening. But did that mean he wouldn't have met Ali?

He dismissed the thought as soon as it hit.

Braden was a small town. One way or another, they'd have met.

And if you'd never decided to hide out in this small town in the first place?

He shoved the question to the back of his mind and pressed *his* knee against hers. "It's my tools that you're really wanting."

She grinned and took another whopping bite of her sandwich, as if she was starving.

Maybe she was. God knew he wanted to take some whopping bites of *her*.

"When do you want to do this? I'll have to run out to the ranch to get 'em."

"I've already promised Marty I'd pull a shift at Magic Jax tonight, so maybe after work tomorrow? I get off at five." The tip of her pink tongue snuck out and caught a drop of au jus from the corner of her lip, causing his mind to immediately jump off the tracks.

He shifted and cleared his throat. "Then I'll meet you at your place a little after five tomorrow. Tools at the ready."

She pointed her sandwich at him. "Real tools. Not… you know."

He gave her a steady look and watched her pupils flare a little. "Pretty sure I can talk you into *you know* as well."

She leaned across the table again, lowering her voice. "My grandmother asked if I was saddle sore! Can you believe it?" She shook her head. "I nearly died." She took another hefty bite of her sandwich.

His encounter with her grandmother had been brief, but somehow he wasn't surprised. "If you don't slow down, you're gonna choke."

She shook her head, chasing the bite with a gulp of water. "Seriously, I'm supposed to be en route from the courthouse. Which is only a whopping ten-minute walk from the department. But I saw your truck in front of the diner and couldn't resist." She grabbed some French fries in one hand and slid out of the booth. She hadn't even taken off her coat in the few minutes she'd been there. She pulled out some crumpled currency and dropped it on the table.

His conscience stirred. "I can get it."

"Don't go all macho on me. Someday when you want to tell me where you get your money to buy cement and paint, you can pay. But for now? It's payday and I like to pay my own way." She quickly swiped her mouth with her napkin and wrapped the French fries in it. Then in front of God and all of Josephine's customers, she leaned over and kissed him boldly on the mouth, her lips all salty and enticing. "I'll see you tonight."

"See you tonight," he said, but she was already hurrying across the diner, stopping short at one of the nearby tables where an old man sat alone, nursing a cup of coffee.

"Well, hello there, handsome! I didn't even notice you were here!"

"Probably 'cause you were a mite busy kissin' that fella." The man's steely gaze traveled to Grant.

But Ali just laughed. "Come in for the liver and onions?"

"You bet."

She looked over her shoulder at Grant. Her eyes were sparkling and she gave him a saucy wink. "Well, you enjoy it." She patted the man's shoulder. "I have to get back on duty."

"Be careful, child."

Both Grant and the old man watched her hurry out of the restaurant. And then the iron-haired guy was looking back at Grant. "She's a good little lady."

That's when Grant placed him. "Squire Clay. From Magic Jax."

"Yep. You're new around here." Squire was definitely taking Grant's measure.

He didn't flinch. "Yes. And she doesn't like being called 'little lady.'"

"No, she does not," he agreed. "She's not quite blood, but she's close, so I'm interested all the same."

"So am I, Mr. Clay."

A smile curled the old guy's lips. Then he lifted his cup in salute. "Good luck to you, then. You're gonna need it with that one."

"Here you go, Squire." Josephine unloaded her tray on the man's table. "While I appreciate you comin' all the way from Weaver for my liver and onions, I *know* Gloria wouldn't approve."

Squire cackled softly. "Man can't live on the leaves and twigs she wants to feed me these days, Josie. Hell, I'm lucky if she feeds me some of my own damn beefsteak once a month!"

Not bothering to hide his amusement, Grant turned to look out the window. He could see Ali jogging across the street, eating her fries and cutting around vehicles moving slowly along the street. The few strands of hair escaping her bun bounced around the shoulders of her coat.

Someday.

History had proven to Grant that thinking of somedays—of futures—was the quickest way to disappointment. If not outright pain. In the service, he'd had to think on his feet. Yeah, there was a lot of planning. But that was always about the mission. About the job.

When it came to his personal life?

"Top off your coffee for you?"

He shook his head, also shaking off the things he didn't want to think about. "No thanks, Josephine." Sleeping at night was hard enough without feeding the caffeine monster all afternoon. The only night since moving into Roger Carmody's house that he'd actually slept without a nightmare had been the one he'd spent with Ali.

He pulled out his wallet, added some cash to Ali's and slid it inside the red vinyl folder Josephine had placed near the edge of the table.

"Need change?"

He shook his head. "All yours."

She slid the folder into the pocket on her apron. "Take your time now. Just let me know if you need anything else."

"Thanks."

She picked up Ali's plate and started to turn away, but hesitated. He automatically braced himself, assuming the worst when she gave him a close look.

"You know, you really *do* remind me of someone," she said. "It's your eyes."

It was his own damn fault for returning to the diner.

"Sorry. Couldn't tell you." He poked at the liver and onions. It was good. But not as good as what Talia used to make back in the day. Before she'd ever gotten sick.

Josephine smiled and shrugged and finally moved away from his booth.

Grant set down his fork, wiped his mouth and slid out of the booth. Before Josephine came back out of the kitchen, he left.

Did she recognize him as T. C. Grant or as Ralph Carmody's bastard grandson?

He didn't know, and didn't have any desire to stick around and find out.

The next night, Ali put on the cocktail-waitress uniform and the dreaded high heels and worked a shift at Magic Jax. But she didn't mind it too much, because Grant sat at the bar nearly the whole time.

"That guy's got it bad for you," Charlene murmured halfway through their shift.

"No, he doesn't." She barely waited a beat before she stole a look at Grant, who was talking with Marty over the soda he'd been drinking all night. "Does he?" Good Lord, she was turning into a teenager.

Charlene just nodded knowingly. "Watch yourself," she warned. "Last guy looking at me like that put babies in my belly and there went all my plans to go to college and get outta this dang town."

Ali had done her stint in college and had no desire to go back. And Charlene was just being Charlene.

She carried the tray of empties she'd been collecting back to the bar and exchanged them for fresh drinks.

Grant caught her eye and smiled slowly.

She swallowed a sudden knot as she lifted the tray. Babies in her belly…

She didn't want to admit what a tempting thought *that* was. Not even to herself.

Maybe it was just the Layla effect.

She delivered the drinks and returned to the bar. "Don't suppose you ever played hockey, did you?"

His eyes narrowed. "Why do I feel like I should ask for some context before I answer?"

"Because you're a smart man." She leaned her hip

against the empty bar stool next to him and absently wriggled her toes inside her shoes. "My grandmother's solution to her annoyance with the Valentine's committee is to throw her own event."

"Hockey?"

She laughed. "Ice skating, actually. She's calling it a Valentine's ball on ice." She felt strangely diffident all of a sudden. "Would you, uh, like to go? You know. With me?"

His lips tilted upward. "You asking me on a date, Officer Ali?"

"I guess I am, Mr. Cooper." She lifted her chin a little. She felt flustered and didn't much care for it. "Well?"

"Maybe he has to check his calendar," Marty interjected from where he stood behind the taps, pulling a beer.

The starch in Ali's shoulders softened.

She rolled her eyes, tucked the round tray beneath her arm and straightened away from the stool.

Grant caught her hand before she could take a step, though. He ran his thumb slowly over the back of her hand and heat climbed sweetly through her veins. "I haven't worn hockey skates in a long damn time. And I've never worn figure skates."

"That makes two of us."

"You played hockey?" His thumb paused over the pulse throbbing in her wrist.

"For a couple years."

"Were you any good?"

"I was all of ten and I could bodycheck with the best of my teammates."

He smiled. "Why am I not surprised?"

"Good grief." Charlene reached between them in

order to grab the basket of peanuts sitting in front of Grant. "Either get on with it, or get a room." She stomped away on her high heels and deposited the basket on a table.

Grant's eyes returned to Ali's. "What's her problem?" His thumb was still pressed against her pulse, which seemed to be speeding up with each breath she took.

"She didn't get to go to college."

His eyes narrowed slightly, hunting for the joke.

"So, you up for a spin around the ice rink or not?"

His eyes drifted to her lips. Then down her body, his glance as warming as a physical touch. "Definitely up."

Ali nearly choked. She tugged her hand away from him and moistened her lips. Then she leaned over and whispered in his ear, "If you still feel that way in an hour, meet me in the storeroom. I've got a fifteen-minute break and the door locks."

His head reared back. Shock, surprise and interest were all in his piercing, aqua eyes. "Officer Ali."

She smiled slightly and turned on her heel, sashaying away.

Chapter Twelve

"Tool man at your service."

Ali knew she had a crazy happy smile on her face, but she didn't care. She opened the front door wider so that Grant could enter. She hadn't seen him since the night before at Magic Jax.

When they'd locked themselves in the storeroom for fifteen glorious minutes.

He was carrying a large red toolbox. And though it was a welcome sight, because it meant she wouldn't have to cave in and call her dad to come to the rescue, it wasn't what caused her to feel so giddy.

That was all on Grant.

"I ordered pizza," she said. "It'll be here in an hour. I hope you like pepperoni and sausage."

He closed the door behind him and set the toolbox on the table near the door. "Only thing I don't like are green peppers." His gaze swept over the empty living room, ending on the clothes draped over their couch. "What's all that?"

"My grandmother's idea of skating attire. She's got this whole Victorian image in her head, I guess. Wants to make sure some of us look the part." She went over and picked up the dark blue coat first. "I can maybe see wearing this. It's sort of cool in a vintage kind of way." She held the wool coat to her shoulders. It had puffy sleeves and nipped in tightly at the waist, then flared out to end below the knee in a wide band of white fur. Fake, she hoped, but when it came to her grandmother, it was dangerous to assume.

She tossed it down and picked up the finely striped yellow-and-white dress that was so long she'd probably catch her skate blades in it and land on her butt. "This, though? There's no way." She spread out the fancily ruffled fabric. "I think it's got a bustle!"

He was grinning as he stopped next to her. He touched the dress. "And I think you'd look real cute in this."

"Oh, come on." She dumped the dress in a heap. "If I'm going to wear that, then you can wear a top hat and…and spats!"

"Might get a little cold without anything covering the areas between. Wear the coat. Make your grandma happy. At least she cares. As for me, I'll skip the spats if you don't mind." He gave her a long look. "We alone?"

Her stomach swooped. "Greer's got a date. She'll be late."

Then he pulled Ali into his arms and kissed her.

Excitement built oh, so fast and oh, so sweetly. But she made herself press her hands against his wide shoulders, and broke the kiss. "No, you don't." She sounded just as breathless as she felt. "I've got a kitchen-faucet situation going nowhere. You can kiss me senseless *after*."

"You're the one leaving me senseless." Amusement filled his deep voice. But he let her go and retrieved the toolbox. "All right. Lead the way, sweetheart."

Sweetheart.

She was afraid she might actually be floating two inches above the floor as she headed into the kitchen.

The towels she'd used to mop up the flood were sitting out of sight in the washing machine. She'd also put away the mop and bucket. Aside from the damp patches still remaining on the unpainted walls, there wasn't a lot of visible damage left. "I shut the water off at the main this morning before I went on duty. On my way home, I stopped at the hardware store. Bobby Don sold me all those parts in the bag there. Said whatever we didn't need, I could return."

"Good deal." Grant set his tools on the floor and glanced in the bag before kneeling down to look under the sink. It wasn't hard, since the cupboard below it possessed no door. "Looks like you've patched this pipe a time or two." He pulled his head out to look at her. "Would've been easier to change out the pipes."

"Yes, yes. You went to the same school that my father did. Point is, we're doing it now." She hugged her elbows. "If I let you play doctor with me later will you save the lecture that I *know* my father would deliver?"

He slanted a look her way and she shivered. "That's a pretty hard bargain you drive, little lady."

She propped her hands on her hips. "Oh. My. God. Do *not* start that up. Squire can get away with it because he's sort of related and he's older than dirt." She jabbed her finger in the air at him. "You, however, are neither."

He chuckled and pulled off his coat, handing it to her.

Then he rolled up the long sleeves of his T-shirt and lay down on his back, working his head and upper torso as far as possible into the sink cabinet. Then he stuck his hand out blindly. "Scalpel, Nurse Ali."

She giggled and flipped open the toolbox. "How'd you learn this home-repair stuff, anyway? It can't possibly all come from books." She handed him a pipe wrench and his hand disappeared beneath the cabinet. He bent one knee as he worked and she swallowed, enjoying the sight of him sprawled there. Her very own Mr. Fix-it.

"Learned a lot from Cal. My dad. And in the service I learned even more. Not just the tech stuff, but how to creatively make an unlivable place a little more livable." He clanged a pipe and a moment later tossed a piece onto the floor by her feet. "There's your problem," he said. "Pipe's rusted right through."

She could see that. She was a long way away from being squeamish, but she picked up the gross pipe with two fingers and pitched it in the trash, then returned to crouch near his knees. "What did your dad do?"

"Retired air force."

Ahh. She smiled, glancing at his midsection where his shirt had ridden up an intriguing inch. It was all she could do not to trail her finger along that wedge of bare skin. She already knew he had a few ticklish spots. And she knew exactly where they were. "You followed in his footsteps?"

"Something like that. I enlisted after 9/11."

"A lot of people did."

He tossed her two more pieces of pipe and came out from the cupboard long enough to grab some new ones from the bag. "He was an honest-to-God hero, though," he said after he'd ducked back beneath the sink. "A PJ."

"Pararescueman? No kidding? I have a cousin who—" She broke off at the sound of the front door opening. "Hold on. Greer's date must have tanked." She pushed to her feet and went to the doorway.

But it wasn't Greer who'd come in. It was Maddie, carrying Layla on her hip.

"Hi!" Ali went over and divested her sister of the baby. "What're you doing here? Where's Linc?"

Maddie peeled out of her coat, then deftly worked off Layla's. "He's outside talking to Mrs. Gunderson. We just came from dinner with Judge Stokes."

Ali froze. "And…?"

"And what do you think? I see you got a delivery from Vivian, too. You going to wear it?" Maddie kicked off her shoes and padded into the kitchen, only to stop short. No doubt because of the sight of half a man sticking out from the kitchen cabinet. "Um, hello?"

"Hello."

Ali slid between Maddie and the doorjamb in time to see Grant sketch a wave with the wrench in his hand.

She sat at the table with the baby on her lap and smiled into Layla's face. The baby was wearing a stretchy footed thing with a green monster on the belly that Ali had bought for her before Christmas. It already looked like it was getting too small. "Grant's replacing the pipes and the faucet."

"That's great." Maddie stepped around his long legs and pulled open the refrigerator. "Got anything edible in here?"

"Pizza'll be here in less than an hour. Manetti's. You know there'll be plenty." The pizzeria only made one size—gargantuan.

Her sister made a face.

"Oh, and since *when* do you not like pizza?"

"Well." Maddie closed the refrigerator door and turned to look at Ali. Her palm settled on her flat stomach.

And just like that, Ali knew. She knew, and delight filled her, along with a sharp little pang that she feared might be envy. "You're pregnant!"

Maddie nodded.

"No *wonder* you've looked like a worn-out rag lately!"

Her sister sputtered a laugh. "Geez, Ali. So flattering."

Envy be damned. She leaned over and set Layla on the floor, with Grant's legs providing a suitable barrier between her and the toolbox, then darted to her sister, pulling her in for a boisterous hug. "Oh, my God. We're getting a baby!"

"Well, don't squeeze it out of her just yet."

Ali looked over to see her brother-in-law in the kitchen doorway. She let go of Maddie to hug Linc, too. "This is *such* great news!"

Grant had pulled himself out from the cabinet and was giving Layla a wary look. "Congratulations." He extended his hand.

"Thanks, man." Linc's eyes were watchful as the two of them shook.

Ali had to remind herself that even though it felt like Grant had been in their lives—*her* life—for a very long time, the reality was something quite different. She quickly introduced them. "Grant Cooper. Lincoln Swift. Maddie's husband."

"You're Layla's uncle."

Grant's expression looked a little tight to Ali. Maybe it was because Layla had decided to explore his legs and was rocking back and forth on her stomach as if she wanted to climb over them. Which would have been a feat, since she hadn't even started crawling yet.

"That's the working theory," he said. He glanced at Ali. "You should probably pick her up, shouldn't you?"

The worn floor had never been so clean, because of the flood from the kitchen pipes yesterday. She briefly entertained the notion of plopping the baby on his belly, just to see what he would do, but ultimately, she leaned down and plucked Layla off the ground to nuzzle her sweet-smelling neck. "Better?"

"Yep." He stuck his head back beneath the cabinet and started clanging around the pipes again.

She was determined not to read too much into his apparent disinterest. It had taken her a while to get comfortable around a baby, too.

She turned her attention back to Maddie. "Have you told Greer yet?"

"I thought she'd be here, too."

"She's got a date."

Ali caught the look that passed between Maddie and Linc and a knot formed inside her stomach. "All right. So we know the good news. Now what's the bad? What did Judge Stokes say?"

Her question seemed to hover in the tense air and the knot doubled in size.

Maddie cupped her hand tenderly over Layla's blonde head. "He said that unless new information about her real mother surfaces, he's going to rule on Layla's final status before the end of the month."

"And what's that mean?" Grant's voice sounded hollow from inside the cabinet.

Ali could see the truth in her sister's eyes. "It means we're all going to lose her," she said huskily. "Just admit it, Maddie. That's what you're saying!"

Maddie bit her lip. Her eyes were damp. She reached for Linc's hand and cleared her throat. "The, uh, the family that's next on the list is being reviewed. My boss is handling it himself. He warned me that they are eminently qualified to adopt. They live over in Jackson, but they have plans to move to Florida, where they have other family. They would have gone already, except that they learned there's a baby who might be available for placement soon."

Ali's eyes burned. "This is *such* bull. Layla should be staying here. We all know it. Aren't you going to fight Stokes, Maddie?"

"How?" Maddie spread her hands. "Everywhere we've turned has brought us to a dead end, Ali."

"But Grant's her uncle! We *know* he is."

Grant slid out from beneath the sink. He sat up. His aqua eyes were unreadable. "Knowing isn't proof."

"And we can't *get* proof. Not until we find your sister. And look what a bang-up job I've done of that!" Frustration twisted inside her. "There's only one thing left to do."

"We're not running off with Layla," Maddie warned.

"And that's the difference between you and me," Ali retorted. "Because I would."

Maddie just looked at her.

Her shoulders fell. "Okay, so I wouldn't. But I'd *want* to."

"You think we don't?" Linc closed his arm around Maddie and she leaned into him.

"I don't care what it looks like to the court," Ali said flatly. "Time is running out. We need—"

"A private investigator," Grant interrupted.

Ali nodded. "Vivian will pay for it. She's offered often enough—"

"Layla's *my* niece." Grant pushed to his feet. "I'll pay for it."

Ali opened her mouth to challenge him. Where on earth would he get the money?

"There's not a court around who would argue with my legitimate right to find my own missing sister." His voice was even. "It doesn't have a damn thing to do with the baby and who has the best claim to her."

"You do have that right," Maddie whispered huskily. "She's your family."

He looked grim. "And I'm probably the worst one for her."

"Grant. That's not true." Ali reached for his hand but he shook her off. And the knot inside her stomach got a whole lot tighter.

"Yeah? Nobody with *my blood* has ever wanted me. Not my mom. She spent years trying to pass me off on guys she'd slept with as their kid, just to get money that she'd usually snort up her nose. And her dad—well, good ol' Roger Carmody said he'd rot in hell before he'd see his family name smeared by a little bastard like me. That's the kind of blood that runs in my veins.

"I'll find Karen and she can answer for what she did—abandoning her own baby. But for Layla's sake, she'd be better off with almost anyone other than me." He dropped his wrench in the toolbox and kicked the lid closed. He looked at Ali; his expression was closed. "Pipes are replaced. All you need to do is fit the new faucet in place and tighten the bolts and connect the supply line." He left the kitchen.

"Wait!" She hurriedly transferred Layla to her sister's arms and followed him. "Where are you going?"

He'd already grabbed his coat and was reaching for the front door. "I need to get out of here."

"But I—" She broke off. Swallowed hard. Her mind was still spinning. Not only because of Layla, but also because of everything he'd said. "I'll come with you, then."

"That's not a good idea."

"Grant, I just… I don't want you to be by yourself."

"I've been by myself nearly my whole damn life, Ali. It's what I'm good at." His eyes skated over her. "And frankly, it's what I prefer."

Then he yanked open the door and went out into the dark.

And all she could do was stand there, watching him go.

"Here." A hand came out of nowhere and set a short, squat glass partially filled with amber liquid in front of her.

Ali wrinkled her nose against the smell of the whiskey and looked up at Greer. "I didn't hear you come in. When did you get home?"

"Little while ago. Maddie called me."

She and Linc had left shortly after Grant had bolted. But that had been hours ago. "What time is it?"

"Little after eleven." Greer pulled out the chair opposite her and sat. She looked at the faucetless sink, but made no comment. "Want to talk about it?"

"Nothing to talk about. There's a ninety-nine-point-nine percent chance that Layla will be adopted by a couple who're moving to *Florida*." She'd never been to the state. Never had reason to hate it. But she did now.

"About Grant."

"Why? So you can tease me for liking a bo-oy?"

Greer just watched her.

Ali groaned. She dropped her head onto her arms atop the table. "I'm sorry. I'm a bitch."

"You're in love."

She whipped her head up so fast it was a wonder she didn't get whiplash. "No, I'm not."

"Anyone denying something that fast is guilty."

"They teach you that in law school?"

Her sister smiled slightly. "You sleep with him?"

She dropped her head back onto her arms. "Like you would not believe."

"Well. I think I'm envious."

"Because this is *so* much fun." She lifted her head again. "I fall for the wrong guy. Every time."

"Every time. As if there have been *so* many." Greer tsked. "Ali. Come on. Who's to say Grant's the wrong guy, anyway?"

"He told me he didn't want me!"

"In those exact words?"

"Yes! Well, no. But it's what he meant."

"Yup. Okay. I see."

"You weren't there. You don't know."

"Maddie was there. She heard. And if she weren't feeling so blasted sick being newly pregnant, she'd be here thumping your head instead of me." Suiting action to words, Greer flicked Ali's head with her finger. Hard.

And it smarted now the same way it had when they were ten. Ali sat up again, rubbing her head. "Maddie doesn't thump anyone's head. She's too nice."

"Unlike me," Greer said tartly.

"Oh, you're nice," Ali said grouchily. "You just hide it under that laywer layer you got going. Maddie's nice on the surface. And you're both brilliant. And I'm—" She made a face. "I'm a glorified meter maid. And not all that glorified, when it comes down to it. I let more people slide on expired meters than not. If the town's budget was dependent on parking fines, Braden would go bankrupt."

"Good grief," Greer muttered. "Exaggerate much?" She reached for the drink and took a sip of it herself. "What I am is too impatient with people who are feeling sorry for themselves."

"I'm not feeling sorry for myself. I'm just facing the truth." She slid the glass out of Greer's hand and tossed it back, wincing when the liquor hit the back of her throat like a blowtorch. "I started thinking maybe we were onto something special." She blamed her hoarseness on the fire burning down her esophagus.

Not that she was in love with him.

"You know what I admire about you, Ali?"

Ali fluffed her streaky brown hair. "My incredible taste in hair color?" She knew Greer had thought she was nuts when she'd done it.

"I have never understood the chip you have on your shoulder." Greer's eyes were annoyed. "The fact that you never quit. Never. You don't give up. On anything. And God knows you don't back down. Even when it would be more advantageous in the long run for you to do so."

Ali jerked back, genuinely surprised.

"So why are you giving up on Grant just because he spewed some claptrap about being better off alone?"

She opened her mouth to argue. But nothing came out.

She stood and went over to the counter. The fancy gooseneck faucet they'd bought months ago was still in its box. She pulled it out and started assembling it.

"You don't have anything to say?"

She fed the faucet line through the hole in the sink and then crouched down. Nuts and bolts. Supply line.

"Alicia!"

She finally sat down on the floor and looked at her sister. "What if he really meant it, Greer? What if he turns me away?"

Greer leaned over and grabbed her hands, squeezing them. "Ali. What if he doesn't?"

Chapter Thirteen

"You need a phone line."

Grant eyed Ali, standing on his porch beneath the bare, flickering lightbulb, and wondered if he'd finally fallen asleep to dream. She was wearing her uniform and coat, but her hair streamed loosely over her shoulders. "Haven't we been here before?"

She watched him. It had started snowing again, and the occasional snowflake floated into the sphere of flickering light. "Are you going to invite me in?"

Last time she hadn't waited for an invitation.

He stepped out of the doorway and she came inside.

There were two more boxes sitting near the door. They'd been there when he came home tonight.

Chelsea's biting idea of humor. Bury him in shipments of his own damn book.

Ali stepped around them. She unfastened her coat but didn't take it off. "You get a lot of books. I never see you read."

"It's two in the morning, Ali. What do you want?"

"Yeah. It's two in the morning. I didn't have to pound on your door to wake you up or anything."

"Waking would require sleeping."

Her lashes were lowered, keeping him from truly seeing what she was thinking. "I wasn't going to come."

He threw himself down on the couch and pinched his eyes shut. "That would have been a good choice."

"What's your story, Grant?"

"I didn't give you enough of it back at your house?" He opened his eyes to see her slowly pace across the floor.

"From what I've been able to piece together," she said in an even tone, "Roger Carmody was a puritanical bastard. Helen Carmody, Roger's wife, appeared to be equally puritanical, though it was common knowledge that Roger was abusive. When she died, their daughter, Denise, was just sixteen. There was a brief investigation into Helen's death and it was ruled suicide." Ali turned to pace the other way. "A few years later, when Denise, now eighteen, came to tell her father that she'd been raped, Roger blamed her. Kicked her out of the house. When Denise learned she was pregnant as a result of that rape and once more went to her father, he turned her away yet again."

His stomach churned. "Guess you've been doing some homework, Officer Ali."

"I wish you would have told me."

"So you can feel sorry for me?"

"So I would have understood you more. Instead, I had to spend the last several hours pumping poor Mrs. Gunderson for details and once again use departmental resources for a personal matter." She stopped pacing. Pushing one of Chelsea's oversize boxes in front of him, she sat on the edge of it, clasping her hands in front of her. "None of what happened with the Carmodys was your fault. You must know that, Grant. Roger's failure as a father *and* a grandfather is not your failure." She hesitated. Waiting.

But he had nothing to say.

"He's dead, you know. After the bank took back the ranch, he went to Minnesota, where he had grown up. Died alone and penniless, living on the street just like he'd condemned his daughter and grandson to do some thirty years earlier."

"I know."

She didn't question how he knew. She merely pulled a piece of paper from her pocket and held it out. "My grandmother gave me the name of an investigator that she's had reason to use before. She says his retainer is pretty high but he always gets results. And she says that now isn't the time for pride. She's happy to pay—"

"I already have an investigator."

Ali slowly returned the paper to her pocket.

"It's the same investigator who told me the glad tidings about Roger. I don't need anyone's money when I've got plenty of my own."

She pushed to her feet, looking disbelieving.

"It's all under the corporation."

"What's all under what corporation?"

"Rules, Inc. My corporation."

He got up and went into the kitchen, returning with a knife.

Her eyebrows rose slightly.

"Don't worry. I'm not gonna use it on you." He sliced open the box and pulled out one of the slick hardbacks stacked tightly inside. He handed it to her and went back to the couch, waiting for the puzzlement in her eyes to shift inevitably to comprehension. Blame would be soon to follow.

She stared at the gold lettering on the glossy black background. "You tried to give me this the day I first came here." She flipped over the book. And there on the back jacket was his photograph. "T. C. Grant." She looked pained. "Right there in front of me this whole time." Instead of heaving the book at his head, which is what he'd have wanted to do if their positions were reversed, she flipped it open and started paging through it. "What's the T.C. stand for?"

"Talia and Cal."

She closed the book and held it against the front of her coat. "Your adoptive parents. That's another blank I couldn't fill in. How did your paths cross? Mrs. Gunderson said when Roger turned away Denise that last time, she didn't stick around here. Rumor had it she hitched a ride out with a trucker heading north. After that—" Ali spread her arms, shaking her head "—all Mrs. Gunderson heard was an occasional rumor that Denise was in Florida. Texas. California. Everyone figured she'd either lost the baby or had an abortion. Not surprisingly, Roger never said anything more about either one of you. So why Oregon?"

"Why not Oregon? We'd been every place else. Denise had a one-nighter with Cal once. Before he and Talia were married. We were in Portland and she was broke. She looked him up, prepared for her usual con. Only this time it didn't work like either one of us expected. He knew I wasn't his kid, but he still offered her twice her normal asking price. In order to get it, though, she had to leave me there."

She sucked in an audible breath.

"She jumped at it. Took the money, told me 'so long' and ran. I never saw her again."

"Grant—"

"I don't want your pity."

"No, you just want to be left alone. So you can... what? Feel sorry for yourself while you make this house habitable again? Is it working? Are you erasing Roger Carmody from this place with every pass of a paint roller?" She spread her arms wide. "Or are you just here to keep reminding yourself that the Carmodys didn't want you?"

"Dammit, Ali—"

"No! Dammit, Grant!" She tossed the book aside. "Their failures aren't *your* failures!"

"Then why did I tell my own sister to stay the hell out of my life!"

Grant's shout seemed to echo around the walls, and Ali sucked in a breath.

He swore and kicked over the box and dozens of black-covered books slid out onto the floor. "I did the same damn thing to her that Roger did to my...to Denise. I shut her out. Cut her off. And she ended up so freaking desperate she dumped her kid off on someone else, too."

Ali slid her arms around his waist and pressed her head against his heart. It was pounding hard.

"Don't."

She linked her fingers together even tighter.

"Goddammit, Ali. I said don't." He tried to push her away, but she hung on like a limpet.

Finally, he stopped pushing and held her back. And only then, when his heart wasn't pounding like a wild beast's and his breath wasn't whistling between his teeth, did she finally ease her grip. "Tell me about Cal and Talia. You said he was a PJ?"

He gave a huge sigh, and it took only a small nudge from her before he dropped unresistingly onto the couch. "It's not gonna work," he said. "Getting me to talk about them doesn't make me forget the rest."

"I have the feeling getting you to talk at all is an accomplishment."

He frowned. "Cal couldn't have kids. That's how he knew Denise's claim was crap. And evidently Talia had a soft spot in her heart for nine-year-old boys who could barely read or write thanks to their upbringing. They hadn't even had Karen a year when I entered the picture."

Ali pulled off her coat and sat next to him. "Obviously you overcame the reading and writing challenges."

"She was an English teacher." He leaned his head back against the couch. "But she quit work once I entered the picture. I did *not* appreciate all of her attention. They had rules I was expected to follow. The only rules I knew up until then were to keep the clerks distracted in stores while Denise shoplifted our next meal and to keep my head down if the cops were too close. With Cal and Talia it was keeping my room clean. I'd never even *had* a room before. I had to say please and thank you. I had to go to school on weekdays. Church on Sundays. It was a helluva change."

"I can only imagine."

"Cal didn't put up with any crap, either. I don't know if I was more afraid of getting kicked out by them or of not getting kicked out by them. I think I pulled every stunt in the book during those first six months."

"You were a boy. You were testing boundaries you'd never had before."

"That's what the therapist they made me see said, too."

As far as Ali was concerned, that didn't take any specialized knowledge. It was obvious.

"Anyway, Cal just got tougher. But no matter what I did, he never threatened to kick me out. I'd been with them eleven months and three days when they sat me down and told me they wanted to adopt me. The court had already made them my guardians. But this was more. They were giving me their name." He looked at her and the color of his eyes was even starker against the shadows under them. "There were no long lists of families anxious to adopt a ten-year-old. Particularly one with a history like mine. Less than a month later, I was officially Grant Cooper. I got a brand-new birth certificate with Cal and Talia listed as my parents." He made a low sound. "They gave me a copy of it and I made a frame for it in school and hung it on my wall. It's still hanging on my wall back in Oregon."

She had to push the words past the lump in her throat. "They sound like they were really good people."

He leaned his head back against the couch and closed his eyes. He nodded once.

"Did they know about T. C. Grant? About your writing?"

"No."

"I'm sure they'd have been very proud."

"Maybe. My mom wasn't particularly happy when I quit college to enlist."

"What were you studying?"

"English education."

The lump got bigger. "You wanted to be an English

teacher?" Like his adoptive mother. The woman who'd helped him learn to read and write.

"Hard to imagine."

She rested her head against his shoulder. "Not so hard," she whispered. Instead of teaching, he'd turned to the military. Like his father. "What was the air force like?"

"Like I'd found another family. Particularly after they were both gone."

"Why didn't you stay in?"

"I left to try to save my marriage. That was a bust."

She remembered his text message from his ex-wife all too vividly. The hearts. The lovey-dovey. "Are you sure?"

He opened his eyes then and looked at her. He gestured at the books. "The only thing Chelsea still wants out of me are words. And I don't have any."

"She likes the books, then."

"She publishes the books," he revealed in a tired voice. "All these boxes she sends me? Her idea of making a point."

"About what?"

"She wants another *CCT Rules* novel. Wants me out on book tours. Look-ee here. Real-life hero, writing about the true-to-life exploits of fictional hero Cal Reid. And it's all bull." He pushed off the couch and kicked one of the books. It skidded wildly across the floor. "She keeps sending 'em just to prove that no matter where I run, I can't get away from *CCT Rules*. She doesn't get that no matter where I am, I can't write. I've tried. And there's nothing there. Not. One. Word. There hasn't been since Seymour died." He kicked another book. And another.

They shot across the floor like weapons.

"Grant."

"He shouldn't have died. *He* was the hero. He stayed with his wife. He loved his kids. But I got out and what happened?"

He kicked yet another book and Ali hastily jumped out of the way.

"I perform what's supposed to be cathartic exercise, and Chelsea's off and running. Suddenly, there's a book and people start thinking *I'm* the hero." He clawed his fingers through his hair. "They start coming out of the woodwork, showing up at my door, telling me about their dads and their moms and their sons and daughters who've paid the ultimate price and think there's some magical way I can make that *better* by knowing their stories. Or writing about 'em. Have Cal Reid, fictional war hero, save their lives at least between the pages of a book. And if it's not those poor souls, it's the women thinking I'm worth a notch on their bedpost just because I've hit a bestseller list or two! Sneaking in my house. Showing up in my bed." He kicked another entire box of books and the cardboard snapped, sounding like a shot. The books poured out of it like an exploding volcano.

He finally went still, wrapping his fingers around the back of his neck. His shoulders were slumped. "All I wanted to do was be able to *sleep* at night," he said gruffly. "That's all I ever wanted to do. After the first book, it was okay. For a long time. But then—" He broke off, shaking his head.

"Seymour died," she ventured softly. She remembered the ivory invitation she'd found in his kitchen drawer that first day. He hadn't made a big deal about it, but that hadn't kept her from reading what it said. *Seymour Reid. Valorous Actions. Award Ceremony.*

He didn't answer and she ached inside. For the little boy he'd been. For the man he'd become.

"I can't do what Cal and Talia did. I can't be a parent to Layla. I don't have what it takes to do the job right."

"How do you know that until you try?"

"Every time I've found something to love, I've lost it. And if I didn't lose it, I kicked it away. Layla deserves more."

"So do you."

He shook his head. He dropped his hands and finally looked at her. His eyes were dark. "Go home, Ali. There's nothing here for you."

She remembered getting thrown by a horse once when she was little. The way her breath had been knocked out of her. The feeling of trying to pull in air and not being able to.

This was worse.

She bent down and picked up one of the books from the floor. The glossy black jacket had been torn and was slipping off the hardback's spine. "I'm an ordinary woman, Grant." The words felt raw. As raw as oxygen sneaking out of stunned lungs. "Living an ordinary life in a small, ordinary town." She held the book up in front of his face. "This sort of thing freaks me out. The hearts and hugs and kisses that your ex-wife texts to you freak me out. The fact that I'm falling in love with you freaks me out. But that doesn't keep me from knowing that everything here is for me. You are for me."

"Ali," he said, his jaw clenching.

"I can't make you believe a thing until you stop looking at what was and allow yourself to hope for what could be. It doesn't have to be with me. It doesn't even have to be with Layla. But please, if only to honor the ones who did get to love you while they could, don't close yourself off from the possibility of having that again. Whether you want to admit it or not, you deserve to be loved. You deserve to be able to love."

"I can't—"

"You mean you won't." She tossed aside the book and picked up her coat. "What do you think a real hero is? Some mythical, perfect, larger-than-life figure? This Cal Reid character you write about? Is it someone who never falters? Is never afraid?" Her voice went raw all over again. "I think a real hero is someone who shows courage despite the odds." Her eyes burned and she pulled open the door. If he saw her cry, he'd blame himself for that, too. "I think a hero is someone who'll face the fear behind *can't* and at least *try*."

Then, without even pulling on her coat, she hurried out into the snowy night.

She made it all the way to the highway before she had to pull over. Not from the snow. But from the tears blinding her. From the fact that he hadn't changed his mind and asked her to stay. From the fear that it was entirely likely that he never would.

Ali dipped the paint roller into the pan and rolled it back and forth, coating it with Svelte Sage. The paint was vaguely green. Vaguely gray. Vaguely brown.

It had taken her and her sisters weeks to agree on the color.

Now, as she lifted the roller from the paint and ran it in a long swathe against the kitchen wall, carefully avoiding the cabinets that one day would be a lovely off-white, she couldn't even remember why that decision had been so darn hard to make.

It had been nearly a week since she'd seen Grant. Since she'd told him she was falling in love with him.

"Falling." Her lips twisted in a frown. "Too late."

"Talking to yourself?"

She looked at Greer, who'd padded barefoot into the kitchen. "I thought you were still at the office. I didn't hear you come in."

"Walked right past you thirty minutes ago, sweetie. Obviously, you were preoccupied."

"Paint will do that to a person." She ran the roller up and down.

"Yeah. Paint." Greer picked up a clean paintbrush and toyed with the bristles. "I'm thinking about quitting my job."

The paint roller jumped right over the edge of the cabinets. "*What?* Why?" Somehow, she'd managed to get paint all over her hands, too.

"Because I feel like I'm not accomplishing anything useful!" Greer tossed down the brush and grabbed a rag, wetting it under the gooseneck faucet before swiping the side of the cabinets. "Shoplifters and drunk drivers and bad-check writers. It seems so pointless. I can't help the people I want to help." She dropped the rag on the plastic sheet that Ali had spread over the table to protect it from paint spatters.

"So what do you want to do? Start working for the prosecutor?"

Greer's lips compressed. "I don't know."

"Join Archer's practice?"

"I don't know," she said again.

Ali didn't know what was worse. Her own personal pity party or the disconcerting sight of her sister not knowing what to do. "You'll figure it out," she said. "You always do." The phone on the wall rang and she automatically reached out to get it, forgetting the paint on her hand. "Hello?"

Greer rolled her eyes and tossed the paint rag toward her.

"Templeton." Sgt. Gowler's voice was abrupt and so unexpected that she automatically feared she'd gotten her days off messed up. "You're gonna want to get in here."

Her shoulders sank. That's what she got for allowing her own misery to so preoccupy her. "I'm sorry, sir. I'll be there as soon as I can."

"Got a hit in Minneapolis on that missing persons for the Cooper woman."

"What?"

"It's not good, Ali."

Her stomach clenched. Gowler never called her by her first name.

"Woman now identified as Karen Cooper was killed in a multivehicle collision on New Year's Eve."

She sank weakly onto a chair, vaguely aware of Greer's concerned face. "That was over a month ago."

"She died as a Jane Doe."

"How do we know it's actually Karen?"

"Friend of hers—roommate—came in to report she'd gone missing. She'd evidently been staying there but the friend was out of town until now. Came back and Karen's stuff was all there, but there was no sign of Karen. Two reports meshed."

"Disposition?"

"Unidentified Doe. County's storing the remains. Collision involved a gas explosion and the fire was pretty damaging."

Ali's stomach churned. "Was there any DNA recovered?"

"Should have been, but there was some complication with it. I don't know what exactly. You can find that out when you come in. She didn't have much in the way of personal effects. From what I understand, the friend has what there is boxed up and ready if there's someone who'll want it."

"There is," Ali said quietly. "I'll be there as soon as I can. Sergeant, thank you for calling me."

"Sort of thing doesn't make any of us happy," he said, sounding gruff. Then he hung up.

Ali slowly did the same.

"What is it?"

"Now I know why it's been so hard to find Karen."

Chapter Fourteen

The memorial service was five days later.

It was held at the Braden cemetery even though there was no body to bury. Just a wooden box of ashes that Ali handed to Grant after the service. She'd wanted to get it to him sooner, but red tape and bureaucracy had gotten in the way. In the end, she'd flown to Minnesota herself to retrieve and transport Karen's remains back to Grant. What should have been simple in theory had involved nearly twenty-four hours of travel.

She'd barely made it back to town in time for the service.

"I'm very sorry for your loss." Her voice was husky. It was only the second time she'd seen him since she'd had the unfortunate task of notifying him of his sister's gruesome death. In all her time with the department, she'd had to make a handful of death notifications. They were never easy.

His had been nearly impossible.

Not even the fact that he'd already received the same news from his private investigator had lessened the burden.

Now, his fingers brushed against hers as he took his sister's ashes.

"Thank you."

The words didn't come from Grant.

They came from the tall, strikingly beautiful blonde standing next to him.

Chelsea. His ex-wife. Of the hearts and kissy-kissy text message and the seemingly endless boxes of *CCT Final Rules*. She'd spoken briefly during the service. Talked about Karen in such a way that Ali hadn't even had the heart to hate her too badly.

But that was then. And now, Chelsea's arm was linked with Grant's, as if she still had that right. That wasn't the worst part. The worst part was Grant allowing it.

Ex-wife for the win.

She didn't know why she didn't just move along. There were other people milling around who clearly expected to extend their condolences to Grant. Jaxon was there, along with more than half the staff at Magic Jax, and there were others. Folks Ali didn't even recognize. "A lot of people came."

"More than we expected," Chelsea answered.

Ali's teeth were set on edge. She imagined herself wearing blinders, where all she could see was Grant, not the woman glued to his side. "I noticed that Judge Stokes came, too."

Grant finally spoke. "Not in an official capacity." He looked at Chelsea. "Would you excuse us, Chels?"

The woman's perfectly painted red lips curved downward. "Of course." She unwound her arm, but before she walked away, she pressed her lips to his cheek. As tall as she was and with the expensive high-heeled leather boots she wore, she didn't even have to stretch up to reach him. Together, the two of them looked like they belonged in a magazine.

Ali watched her walk away. Then she looked back at Grant. At the lipstick his ex-wife had left on him. "How are you doing?"

He looked down at the box he held. "I've had better days."

Despite everything, her heart squeezed. "I'm so sorry it ended this way." She pressed her gloved hand against the wooden box. It had started out as a cardboard one. Much like a shoebox. She'd charged the finely carved wooden urn on her credit card. As far as she was concerned, Grant never needed to know about the shoebox.

"She was on her way back here." His eyes were more blue than aqua today. Maybe they were reflecting the pale blue sky. "That's what John—my investigator—thinks, anyway. I'm not so sure, considering she left what few belongings she had behind."

"I wasn't able to speak with her friend who reported her as missing." Ali had tried, but hadn't been able to reach her. If she'd pursued it any further, she wouldn't have made it back in time for the service. "Did you?"

"John did. The friend wasn't all that much of a friend. She had only known Karen for a couple of months. Didn't know anything about her past or whether she'd had a baby. They met because they were both waitressing at the same place. Mostly, she was concerned about collecting the rent that Karen owed. She wouldn't release Karen's stuff until John paid her."

Charming. "You received her belongings, though?"

"Two days ago. She had a few childhood pictures."

"Anything of Layla?"

He shook his head.

Short of a birth certificate, photos of Layla would have helped. Even though they had now located Karen, they were no better off legally establishing her identity as the baby's mother. No better off establishing Grant as her uncle. Even though the medical examiner's office had retained some of Karen's DNA after her terrible end, their bad luck had persisted. The samples had been accidentally damaged, to such a degree that they were useless in trying to match Karen to Layla. Ali would have had a hard time believing it, if she hadn't spoken with the medical examiner's office herself.

"She had a Wyoming driver's license. Nobody knows why she wasn't carrying it with her, but it probably would have burned up in the crash, anyway. A few rings. John thinks one of 'em looks like a wedding ring."

She looked at him sharply. "If she was married, maybe we can find out to whom."

"Sure. Because looking for one needle in the haystack isn't enough."

He was right, but that didn't mean she wouldn't start searching. "Anything else in her things?"

"A couple of rodeo magazines." His lips formed a thin line for a moment. "A couple of novels."

She folded her arms over her chest, shivering. Not from cold. "T. C. Grant novels?" He didn't have to answer when she could see the truth on his face.

It was so painful to see that she had to look away.

But that only brought Chelsea back into her line of sight. She was speaking with a much shorter, plump woman who had two gawky teenagers with her. The fact that Chelsea hugged the other woman made Ali think she was more likely a friend from their shared past than a friend of Karen's.

"How long were the two of you married?"

"Seven years. Six and a half too long."

She raised her eyebrows. "Yet you worked with her on the books. And she's here now."

"I told you," he said, his expression darkening. "She thinks she can twist another book out of me."

"She sounded like she genuinely cared about Karen."

"She did. Maybe enough to want to be here today, but Chelsea's nothing if not practical. Come to a memorial service. Try and bribe a man into her publishing clutches at the same time."

Chelsea was heading back their way and Ali had no desire to come up short—literally—next to her. "If you ask me, she looks like she's got an interest in keeping her clutches on you in all sorts of ways." Ali pulled off her glove to wipe her finger against his sharp, angular jaw. She showed him the red color that she came away with. "She's certainly leaving her mark." She rubbed the lipstick away on her glove and pulled it back on. "I should go. Vivian's Valentine's ball is tomorrow."

A whisper of a smile lit his face for just a moment. "Going to wear the bustle?"

Her throat tightened. "Still debating that," she responded in a credibly dry tone. Then she gave Chelsea what she thought was a polite nod and she walked away.

"That's her."

Grant barely listened to Chelsea. He was too busy watching Ali walk away.

"Her grandmother is Vivian Archer Templeton," Chelsea went on.

"So?"

His ex-wife huffed a little. "So, she's one of the wealthiest women in the country."

"Good for her."

"She asked if my company would consider donating to the library she's trying to get built."

He looked down at the box. At Karen. He should feel more grief. Except that he'd been preparing himself for this moment for years. "You knew Karen as well as I did. Do you think she was capable of abandoning her baby?"

Chelsea didn't hesitate. "Yes." She squeezed his arm. "I also think she was capable of immediately regretting it, but as usual didn't have a clue about how to make it right. Karen was an adult, Grant. She was always responsible for her own decisions. Including forging your name on that contract."

He gave her a sharp look. "You *knew*? And never said squat?"

"I didn't know at first. And I stayed quiet for the same reason you did."

"Another *CCT Rules* book."

Her lips tightened. "To protect Karen. You know, I'm happy to ride the money train, but if you don't want to write another, then don't. Write something else. Or finish your teaching degree. Or pretend you actually want to live in your grandfather's house. Whatever. I'd actually rather see you happy for once." She nodded toward Ali, who'd nearly reached her departmental SUV. "Her grandmother told me how much she went through to get Karen back to you. Above and beyond, if you ask me."

"What are you talking about?"

So she told him.

"I didn't think she could do it, but I was wrong." Meredith stood next to Ali and Greer on the short end of the oval ice-skating rink, where at least two dozen skaters were circling the perimeter to the old-timey music playing from a loudspeaker. The sound quality was somewhat scratchy, which only seemed to add to the ambiance.

"What I don't get," Greer added, "is why so many people were willing to get dolled up in clothes like these." She plucked at her outfit, which was equally as fussy as Ali's. "Look at Archer." She gestured at their big brother, who was wearing a long coat—a frock coat, according to Vivian—narrow trousers and a top hat. He carefully escorted Vivian around the edge of the ice. "Even he got into the spirit."

"He just wanted to make Vivian happy," Ali murmured. But Greer had a point. There were more skaters who were dressed in old-fashioned outfits than in jeans and jackets.

"Well, I like to dress up now and then, but this is ridiculous. Maddie should be glad she's feeling so crummy with morning sickness and had a good reason to be able to stay home." Greer grabbed handfuls of her dress, making sure it was clear of her skates, and stomped off toward the warming hut, which was actually an extremely large heated party tent, where even more people were hanging out, drinking and eating and having a grand time if the decibel level of the conversation was anything to go by.

"Does Greer seem particularly edgy to you?"

"I think she's as frustrated as we all are with Layla's situation," she murmured. "I'm going to get some hot chocolate. Can I bring you one?"

Meredith beamed. She looked especially lovely with a dark purple coat that was similar to Ali's and a furry white muff. "I'd love some, sweetie. Oh, I wish your dad was here. He would've seen that his mother isn't as terrible as he still wants to believe." She stepped onto the edge of the ice and waved her hand toward Archer as he and Vivian approached.

Ali waited a moment, smiling at the sight of her mother and brother and grandmother all skating together. She wished she could feel the smile deeper than just the surface, though.

She followed the path to the warming hut and walked inside. She was wearing the white figure skates that her grandmother had provided along with the clothing, and walking around in them was making her ankles hurt. Maybe she wouldn't notice so much if she was skating, but since Grant was supposed to have been her date before everything had exploded around them, she didn't really have the heart or the desire to get on the ice.

She joined the people in line at the closest refreshment station. There were four such stations, all positioned in the corners of the tent like open bars at a wedding reception. And next to each one, there was a tall standing mirror, along with more piles of costumes and an old-fashioned photo booth, where people could get their pictures taken. She knew that had been Delia's idea. Her cousin was flitting around from corner to corner, making certain that everyone was having a grand time.

From what Ali could see, most were. She even spotted Hayley and Seth in the far corner, mugging for the camera. Her eldest sister didn't have skates on her feet, Ali noted. Probably because she was a million months pregnant and Seth had an overprotective streak about two miles wide.

As she waited in line, her thoughts drifted to Grant. And to his sister. It had been years since he'd spoken with Karen and that left a lot of time in which she could have married someone. Of course, it was a big if that she had been married in the first place. But if there'd been a husband, maybe even at the time of Layla's birth—

"I like the bustle."

Ali's wandering thoughts screeched to a standstill.

She slowly turned to see Grant behind her. "Hi." The word sort of oozed out of her, more breath than voice. She looked past him, more than a little certain that Chelsea wouldn't be too far away. "I didn't expect to see you here."

"I don't think we ever officially canceled our date."

She chewed the inside of her cheek on that one. "I figured after what we said the other night, it was pretty official." She rocked slightly on her ice skates. The floor inside the tent was made of thick, firm rubber that couldn't be damaged by skate blades.

"Well, regardless. Eva and Emi wanted to come. They saw the signs in the window at Josephine's when we went there after the service yesterday." He lifted his shoulder. He was in the minority when it came to dress. First off, he had boots on his feet rather than skates. He wore dark blue jeans, a tan sweater that looked as soft as cashmere—and probably was—and a black leather jacket.

He looked delicious and handsome and entirely out of her reach.

"Who are Eva and Emi?"

"My goddaughters." He gestured toward the thick, transparent tent panels on the sides of the tent that kept it from feeling too closed-in. "They're out there skating somewhere with Claudia."

"That's nice." She had no clue exactly who he was talking about. "Goddaughters, though. That's a little surprising."

"They're Seymour's kids."

She went still.

"Even though they never met Karen, they came to pay their respects. Because it was what Seymour would've done. They're staying with me out at the ranch."

Her chest felt tight. "That's… I'm glad. Glad you're not alone."

"Seymour was my best friend. Someday I'll tell you all about him. But he wasn't what you would call particularly smart with money."

"I'm not sure where you're going with this," she said faintly, "but okay."

"I'm going to give his family the ranch."

She inhaled. "Oh."

"They'll never need to worry about a roof over their heads. And it's long past time I did more than send them money at Christmas and birthdays. Once the ceremony's over, when they give Claudia Sey's Distinguished Service Cross, I'll make the arrangements to move them. I'll have to get the rest of the house fixed up for them, but—"

She slid her arms around his neck and kissed him. His lips were cool. Firm. He was unquestionably surprised by her move.

Just as abruptly, she backed away again. Her face felt hot. "I think that's a wonderful idea," she said softly. He'd be putting Roger Carmody's ghost to rest for sure.

She realized the line in front of her had disappeared and quickly stepped forward to fill two cups with hot cocoa. "My mother's waiting for me," she said huskily when she tried to move away from the table only to find him standing in her way.

"Did you mean it? What you said the other night?"

She'd said a lot of things the other night. But there

was no question what he meant. Lying was impossible. "Yes."

He lifted the cups out of her hand and set them on the table, then pulled her to the side. Toward the tall mirror. His eyes met hers in the reflection. "What do you see?"

Heartbreak. "I don't know what you want me to say, Grant."

"I want you to say that you see it."

"See *what*?"

He lowered his head until his lips were near her ear. "The mark."

"What are you talking about?"

"The mark," he said again. "You've left it all over me."

She went still.

"Chelsea isn't here," he said quietly. "Not in Braden. Not in my heart. And when she was, she was never as deep as you've gotten since you first pounded your fist on my front door. Your mark is all over me, Officer Ali. And I don't want to rub it off, even if I could. I want to be the man that you think I am. I want to at least try."

Her eyes flooded.

"I'm still a writer with no words, sweetheart. Still a guy who has nightmares more often than not. I'm so far from being the kind of man you deserve that you should walk away and keep going, but the thought of you actually doing that is the one thing I don't think I can survive. Not now. Not after everything that's happened. I know how hard you worked to bring Karen back to me. And I want an ordinary life with an extraordinary woman." His husky voice dropped a notch. "So tell me. Can you see the mark now?"

She exhaled shakily and lifted her fingers to graze

his jaw where Chelsea's lipstick had been. "I think I see it here."

He caught her fingers in his and kissed them. "It's here." He pressed her hand against his chest. His heart.

Tears slid over her lashes. She stared into his aqua eyes. "What do we do now?"

"I don't know," he murmured, lowering his mouth toward hers. "But as long as we do it together, I know we're on the right track. I know it's fast, but my dad always said that just because something was fast didn't mean it wasn't real." He slid his arms around her and pulled her close. "And nothing has ever felt more real than this. I love you, Ali. I never thought I'd say those words again, much less feel them, and I'll spend the rest of my life trying to prove that I deserve you."

Her heart cracked wide. Right then and there. Just fell right open to him. "You don't have to prove anything," she said softly. "You just have to love me."

He slowly smiled. "I think I can manage that."

"Well, can you manage to move it off to the side so some of us who want to use the photo booth *can*?"

Ali and Grant looked over to see Charlene from Magic Jax.

"Better watch yourself," she went on, giving Ali a broad wink. "Babies in the belly." Hauling on the arm of her gangly tall husband, she dragged him toward the photo booth.

Grant pressed his lips against Ali's ear. "What was that about babies?"

She smiled and tightened her arms around him. "I'll tell you all about it later," she promised. "For now…"

His eyebrows went up as he waited for her to finish.

She looked past him to the skating rink beyond the tent. "For now, I want to meet these goddaughters of yours. And then I want to get on the ice and skate with you. My grandmother assures me it's *magical*."

He laughed softly, wrapping his hand with hers. "Well, then. Let's go make some magic."

Epilogue

The glow of the bonfire could be seen for half a mile.

Grant sat huddled on the porch with his arm around Ali and watched it burn.

"I'm glad you decided to donate the books to the local veteran organizations," Ali commented. "I would've felt wasteful burning them all. I mean, Cal Reid seemed to deserve more."

"Yeah, well, he's getting more. I'm also donating to your grandmother's library fund." He linked his fingers with hers. He still couldn't believe he wasn't burning the books. For that matter, he still couldn't believe he had this particular woman at his side.

Just went to prove that miracles could happen.

Maybe enough miracles to get him writing again.

"What do you know about Cal Reid, anyway?"

"He's named after your dad and your best friend. He always gets his man." She bumped her shoulder against his. "Or woman." She gave him a look. "Timmy loaned me his copies of the whole series. I had to swear an oath that I'd return them in perfect condition. They're good, Grant. Really good. Particularly *Final Rules*, even though I know how you felt about writing it." She looked out at the bonfire again. They were burning the wall he'd taken down upstairs to make two small bedrooms into a larger bedroom for Eva and Emi. They'd built the fire well away from the barn so that even if the sparks should fly, they wouldn't do any damage.

Until he'd decided to give the ranch to Claudia and her daughters, he wouldn't have cared if the whole thing went up in flames.

Now, he cared.

He lifted the last item to toss on the fire. "Do you want to do the honors, or shall I?"

She cautiously took the thick, catalog-style envelope and looked inside. She lifted out the junk mail and circulars inside and he felt her relax. "I thought I was going to find an unfinished manuscript in here or something."

"Just Karen's mail that Chelsea had been collecting. She told me there was nothing important in it, so I don't know why she didn't get rid of it herself. But—" He shrugged. "More fuel for the bonfire."

Ali was still pouring stuff out on her lap, occasionally holding a piece of mail up to the light to read. "Some of these things go back years!" She upended the envelope entirely and a last thin piece of mail floated out. She caught it in her hand. "I should have thought to get marshmallows," she said. "A bonfire without marshmallows is kind of a sad thing."

"Next time."

"Why *do* you suppose Karen used the name Daisy

Miranda instead of her own?" She tore open the envelope and looked inside.

"She liked old Carmen Miranda movies. Daisy was the name of the cat she had when we were kids. Why she put the two together is anyone's guess."

"You put Cal and Reid together. She put two things she loved together…" Her voice trailed off. "Grant. This is Karen." She held up a small color photograph of his sister and a man wearing a cowboy hat.

He glanced at the picture. "Yep." He slid his hand beneath her sweater. "What do you say we take this inside?"

"You don't know who the man is with her?"

He sighed faintly and looked more closely at the photograph. "Nope."

"You see what he's doing?"

"Kissing her hand."

"He's kissing the *ring* on her hand." She flipped the photograph over and went still.

He looked.

"So much for vows" had been scrawled on the back.

She pawed through the pieces of mail strewn over the porch beside her. "Here!" She pounced on one and lifted it to the light. "This was postmarked last February. The return address is right here." She stood and the mail scattered as she waved the envelope at him. "Your sister *was* married. Her husband—" she stopped waving to peer at the envelope again— *"Ryder Wilson* mailed this from right here! A year ago. You know what this means?"

"The haystack just got a lot smaller."

She smiled brilliantly and kissed his lips. "The haystack doesn't even exist. This Wilson guy is surely Layla's father! Judge Stokes needs to see this. I know he'll hold off ruling on Layla a little longer while we track down Wilson."

"You're crediting my wild sister with pretty traditional behavior," he cautioned. "Being married to the father of her child."

"At least it's a possibility. Even you must admit that." Her eyes were sparkling. She was extraordinary, and he couldn't believe his good luck.

"Thank you," he said.

"For what?"

"For believing in possibilities. For pounding on my door." He wrapped his arms around her. "For never giving up. I love you, Ali Templeton."

She softened against him. "And I love you, Grant Cooper."

* * * * *

Don't miss the third Templeton triplet Layla's story,

THE RANCHER'S CHRISTMAS PROMISE

by New York Times *and* USA TODAY
bestselling author Allison Leigh

Available October 2018
From Harlequin Special Edition

And be sure to pick up
these other titles from Allison Leigh's
long-running RETURN TO THE DOUBLE C *series:*

THE RANCHER'S DANCE
COURTNEY'S BABY PLAN
A WEAVER PROPOSAL
A WEAVER VOW
A WEAVER BEGINNING
A WEAVER CHRISTMAS GIFT
ONE NIGHT IN WEAVER
THE BFF BRIDE
A CHILD UNDER HIS TREE
YULETIDE BABY BARGAIN

Available from Harlequin Special Edition

Get 4 FREE REWARDS!

We'll send you 2 FREE Books plus 2 FREE Mystery Gifts.

Harlequin® Special Edition books feature heroines finding the balance between their work life and personal life on the way to finding true love.

FREE
Value Over
$20

YES! Please send me 2 FREE Harlequin® Special Edition novels and my 2 FREE gifts (gifts are worth about $10 retail). After receiving them, if I don't wish to receive any more books, I can return the shipping statement marked "cancel." If I don't cancel, I will receive 6 brand-new novels every month and be billed just $4.99 per book in the U.S. or $5.74 per book in Canada. That's a savings of at least 12% off the cover price! It's quite a bargain! Shipping and handling is just 50¢ per book in the U.S. and 75¢ per book in Canada*. I understand that accepting the 2 free books and gifts places me under no obligation to buy anything. I can always return a shipment and cancel at any time. The free books and gifts are mine to keep no matter what I decide.

235/335 HDN GMY2

Name (please print)

Address   Apt. #

City   State/Province   Zip/Postal Code

> Mail to the **Reader Service:**
> **IN U.S.A.:** P.O. Box 1341, Buffalo, NY 14240-8531
> **IN CANADA:** P.O. Box 603, Fort Erie, Ontario L2A 5X3

Want to try two free books from another series! Call 1-800-873-8635 or visit www.ReaderService.com.

"What's going on here, Griffin?"

"I'm on an amazing date with an amazing woman and—"

"This isn't a date," she interrupted, tugging her hand from his.

He shifted, looking down into her gray eyes. Strands of lights lined the pier, so he could see that her gaze was guarded...serious. Not at all the easygoing, playful woman who'd sat across from him at dinner.

"You're sure?"

"I'm not sure of anything at the moment. You might remember my life turned completely upside down last week. But even if that wasn't a factor, I can't imagine you wanting to date me."

"I'm not the same guy I used to be."

She laughed softly. "I get that you were an angry kid and the whole 'rebel without a cause' bit."

"I hated myself," he admitted softly. "And I was jealous of you. You were perfect. Everyone in town loved you. It was clear even back then that you were the golden girl of Stonecreek, which meant you represented everything I could never hope to be."

"But now I'm okay because my crown has been knocked off?"

"That's not it," he said, needing her to understand. He paced to the edge of the pier then back to her. "I can't explain it but there's a connection between us, Maggie. I know you feel it."

She glanced out to the ocean in front of them. "I do."

"I think maybe I realized it back then. Except you were younger and friends with Trevor and so far out of my league." He chuckled. "That part hasn't changed. But I'm not the same person, and I want a chance with you."

"It's complicated," she said softly. "A week ago I was supposed to marry your brother. If people in town caught wind that I'd now turned my sights to you, imagine what that would do to my reputation."

The words were a punch to the gut. He might not care what anyone in Stonecreek thought about him, but it was stupid to think Maggie would feel the same way. She was the mayor after all and up for reelection in the fall. He stared at her profile for several long moments. Her hair had fallen forward so that all he could see was the tip of her nose. She didn't turn to him or offer any more of an explanation.

"I understand," he told her finally.

"I had a good time tonight," she whispered, "but us being together in Stonecreek is different."

"I get it." He made a show of checking his watch. "It's almost eleven. We should head back."

Her shoulders rose and fell with another deep breath. She turned to him and cupped his jaw in her cool fingers. "Thank you, Griffin. For tonight. I really like the man you've become." Before he could respond, she reached up and kissed his cheek.

Don't miss
Falling for the Wrong Brother *by Michelle Major,*
available September 2018 wherever
Harlequin® *Special Edition books and ebooks are sold.*

www.Harlequin.com

THE WORLD IS BETTER WITH

Romance

Harlequin has everything from contemporary, passionate and heartwarming to suspenseful and inspirational stories.

Whatever your mood, we have a romance just for you!

Connect with us to find your next great read, special offers and more.

f /HarlequinBooks

🐦 @HarlequinBooks

www.HarlequinBlog.com

www.Harlequin.com/Newsletters

H HARLEQUIN®

A *Romance* FOR EVERY MOOD™

www.Harlequin.com